W9-BIM-996

FATAL VISION

All of Frank's attention was on the road before him, so he barely noticed a churning sound erupting from a stand of aspens off to one side.

He turned when the sound got louder and saw a car come barreling into view—flashing straight at the pickup!

Frank tried to brake, tried to turn aside. But the onrushing car caught him broadside, smashing him off the road, into the ditch.

The last thing Frank remembered was his own brother, grim-faced at the wheel, ramming him!

Books in THE HARDY BOYS CASEFILES® Series

Available from ARCHWAY Paperbacks

Most Archway Paperbacks are available at special quantity discounts for bulk purchases for sales promotions, premiums or fund raising. Special books or book excerpts can also be created to fit specific needs.

For details write the office of the Vice President of Special Markets, Pocket Books, 1230 Avenue of the Americas, New York, New York 10020.

THE HARDY BOYS No. 11

CASEFILES

BROTHER AGAINST BROTHER

FRANKLIN W. DIXON

AN ARCHWAY PAPERBACK
Published by POCKET BOOKS
New York   London   Toronto   Sydney   Tokyo

This book is a work of fiction. Names, characters, places and incidents are either the product of the author's imagination or are used fictitiously. Any resemblance to actual events or locales or persons, living or dead, is entirely coincidental.

AN ARCHWAY PAPERBACK *Original*

An Archway Paperback published by
POCKET BOOKS, a division of Simon & Schuster, Inc.
1230 Avenue of the Americas, New York, N.Y. 10020

Copyright © 1988 by Simon & Schuster, Inc.
Cover artwork copyright © 1988 Brian Kotzky
Produced by Mega-Books of New York, Inc.

All rights reserved, including the right to reproduce
this book or portions thereof in any form whatsoever.
For information address Pocket Books, 1230 Avenue
of the Americas, New York, N.Y. 10020

ISBN: 0-671-63082-2

First Archway Paperback printing January 1988

10 9 8 7 6 5 4 3

THE HARDY BOYS, AN ARCHWAY PAPERBACK and
colophon are registered trademarks of Simon & Schuster, Inc.

THE HARDY BOYS CASEFILES is a trademark
of Simon & Schuster, Inc.

Printed in the U.S.A.

IL 7+

BROTHER AGAINST BROTHER

Chapter
1

"SURPRISE!" JOE HARDY shouted, whipping an Uzi submachine gun from the cart he was pushing.

The two hijackers froze in the middle of the airplane aisle. A moment before they had thought he was one of them—a terrorist sneaking aboard the plane disguised as a food handler.

Now Joe and his brother, Frank, had dropped their disguises. They were really there to stop the hijacking and rescue Frank Hardy's girlfriend, Callie Shaw.

"We're all going to die!" a terrified passenger screamed.

"Not if I can help it," Joe Hardy said. "Drop those guns, you two."

But the terrorists didn't throw down their weapons. The dark-haired terrorist curled his lip,

1

raised his Uzi, and began shooting. His blond comrade followed suit.

Screams rose, echoing wildly in the confined space of the plane.

Bullets came flying past Joe. It seemed as though an army was shooting. There were more bullets than two machine guns could fire. Miraculously, nothing hit him—in spite of the fact that he was right out in the open.

Joe knew he had to stop these guys. He leveled his gun in a firing position. But when he pulled the trigger, nothing happened. The Uzi was jammed!

More bullets tore past him—a storm of lead. Joe could hear screaming behind him—people were being hit. "Somebody help us!" a woman shouted. "Please!"

Joe couldn't help, though. He stood facing the terrorists, desperately trying to get his gun to work.

But his fingers were clumsy. He fumbled with the bolt of the gun, watching it slip out of his sweaty grasp.

Then a familiar voice cried out behind him. Joe did turn for a second and saw Callie Shaw staggering in the aisle. She had one hand over her shoulder—small streams of red ran between her fingers.

Joe stared at her dumbly, while his brother Frank was yelling, "Callie! You're hit!"

Frank jumped to help her as the storm of bullets increased. Both Callie and Frank fell to the floor, chopped down by the enemy's fire.

"No!" The word was torn from Joe's throat. *"NO!"*

He threw away his useless gun, balled his hands into fists, and charged at the terrorists.

They were still shooting, foot-long flames jetting from the muzzles of their Uzis. Yet none of their bullets touched Joe.

Just as he was almost on top of them, the terrorists stepped aside, revealing a third man.

He was middle-aged, with thinning hair and a pudgy face. Joe recognized him—the leader of the gang. The man grinned an evil smile and held out his right hand.

In it was a bomb detonator!

Joe leapt at him, but the head terrorist pressed the firing button.

"Fool!" was the last word Joe heard before the plane exploded. It all made a terrible sort of sense to Joe. Frank and Callie were gone. And now he was going up in a ball of flame, just as his girlfriend Iola had when a terrorist car bomb had exploded.

Joe stiffened and felt himself being flung into the air. And then . . .

"Sir, sir, wake up."

Joe's eyes opened to meet those of a young woman in uniform.

"Sir, please. We're about to land."

Joe realized that every muscle in his body was

rigid. His blond hair was damp with sweat. He forced himself to relax, shaking his head. "What's going on?"

"Sorry to bother you. You must have dozed off. Please bring your seat to an upright position. We're about to land in Denver."

Joe looked down at his hands. They were still gripping the armrests. "Right," he said, pushing the button to adjust the seat.

The flight attendant walked away. Joe shook his head again and yawned. What a weird dream! he thought. I wonder if the airline food brought it on.

He tried one last time to shake the nightmare away. It was like a horror-show version of their rescue of Callie from hijackers in a recent case, *Hostages of Hate*. So much could have gone wrong. . . . Joe shuddered. He hoped the dream wasn't a bad omen for his present mission.

"That movie put you to sleep?" his neighbor, an overweight businessman, asked.

"Guess so," Joe said. "How did it turn out?"

"Typical Hollywood ending. The guy killed about three thousand bad guys, then rescued a pretty girl from hideous aliens just before the spaceship crashed into San Francisco Bay. The special effects were awful, just awful. The head alien looked like a bicycle covered with carpet."

The businessman put a small calculator and note pad into his briefcase.

"What time is it?" Joe asked.

The man showed Joe an expensive Swiss watch. ''Remember, though, we've traveled across two time zones. Denver's on Mountain Time, two hours earlier than this.'' The businessman straightened his tie. ''You have family here?''

''No,'' Joe told him.

''Out here on business then?''

Joe eyed the man. Was he being friendly—or maybe a little too nosy? ''It's mostly a pleasure trip,'' he finally said.

''Well, the mountains are beautiful, that's for sure.''

Joe glanced out the window and saw beyond Denver to the blue foothills, and beyond them, the white peaks of the majestic Rockies filling the horizon.

''I couldn't help but hear you mutter in your sleep,'' the businessman told Joe.

''Is that right?''

The heavyset man nodded. ''I couldn't make out what you were saying. But it sounded like a girl's name. Ilene. Elaine. Olive. Something like that.''

Joe's breath came in with a little hiss. ''Iola?'' he said.

''Yeah, that sounds right. She your sweetheart?'' the businessman asked with a nudge and a wink.

Again, the image of a ball of fire flashed through Joe's mind. This wasn't a nightmare,

5

though. Iola had really disappeared when the Hardys' car exploded—and Joe had been helpless to save her. "Iola was—special," Joe answered, almost in a whisper. "But she's no longer in my life."

"Well, girls are like buses," the man said, not understanding. "If you miss one, another will be along in a few minutes."

Not willing to set the guy straight, Joe tightened his seat belt, and as the plane began its gentle descent, leaned back in his seat.

He turned his head toward the window, trying not to think about Iola. About what a dangerous place the world had become. The skyscrapers of downtown Denver, surrounded by miles of streets and houses, filled his view. For a moment, as the plane descended, the mountains disappeared behind buildings and the horizon.

The mountains. What a perfect place to hide. He turned his head away from the window and thought about his mission. Later that day he'd be in the Rockies, searching for a man on the run.

The man had been in a witness protection program. But his cover was broken, and he had been running from hit men ever since. His only contact was Fenton Hardy, Joe's private investigator father.

The witness trusted only Fenton Hardy. They maintained a thin line of contact—one that Fenton had to use right then. Apparently, the underworld killers were getting very close to their target. Joe's job was to deliver a coded warning to the witness while Fenton pursued the killers.

The jet's wheels touched down, screeching as rubber hit the concrete runway. Joe felt himself lurch forward slightly. The engines roared as they were reversed to slow the jet. Then the airplane began to taxi toward its gate.

"Ladies and gentlemen," a flight attendant said over the P.A. "Welcome to Denver's Stapleton International Airport. We hope you've had a comfortable flight. And we wish you a pleasant stay here in Denver or wherever your eventual destination will be. Think of us the next time you need air travel, and have a good day."

The airplane rolled to a stop. Passengers leapt to their feet, scrambling to reclaim coats or luggage from overhead compartments. Several people, late for connecting flights, pushed toward the exit.

Joe waited for the bulk of the people to clear out, quietly tapping a finger against the rubber heel of his hiking boot. Hidden inside it was a small plastic capsule housing the message he had to deliver.

The plan was not without danger. Joe was to drive to a remote spot in the Rockies to meet the witness, a man he had never seen. What if Joe did his part, only to be met by hit men?

Maybe it was a hangover from his nightmare, but Joe suddenly felt anxious. He glanced around the cabin. Could the hit man possibly be on board? Could he be one of the flight attendants, even the guy sitting beside him?

"After you," the overweight businessman said, stepping back to make room for Joe in the aisle.

Joe moved in front of the man, almost expecting a weapon to be stuck into his back.

"You take care, now," the businessman said, gently nudging Joe toward the exit. His words sounded like a grim joke. "Take *good* care."

Chapter

2

AT THE AIRPORT Joe picked up a rental car, which Fenton had reserved. "Typical," Joe grumbled as he revved the motor. "They stick me with the least expensive—and least powerful—car in the lot. I'll probably have to *push* this thing uphill!"

Still, it was a beautiful, clear afternoon, a perfect day for cruising toward the Rockies.

The air was dry and a bit thin. Joe noticed that he had the slightest bit of difficulty in breathing because he was almost a mile above sea level. He remembered reading a newspaper article on how more and more athletes were coming to Colorado to train their bodies—and lungs—for the Olympics and other events.

Leaving the airport, Joe got on the interstate heading west and drove past Denver's downtown area. Not as impressive as New York or Chicago, he decided. Still, a dozen or so skyscrapers glistened in the sun.

West of the city limits, the flat plains crowded with suburban houses gave way to rolling hills. As he drove on, the road gradually inclined. Heavy trucks had to downshift to maintain their speed, and Joe passed them, pressing the accelerator pedal to the floor.

Joe noticed a sign for a point of interest just ahead. He checked the car clock—he was ahead of schedule, so he decided to pull off and see it.

Apparently, to build the highway, a large hill had been blasted. The remaining slopes on either side of the road were laid bare as if a piece had been sliced out of a cake.

His car rolled to a stop, and Joe looked up at the impressive road cut. Layer upon layer of geologic history lay exposed. A section of sandy-colored rock was wedged up against a black coal vein, which was wedged up against a thick level of brown stone.

A display explained that the site was an excellent example of the upturning of sedimentary layers, which happened some sixty-five million years before, when the present Rockies were formed.

In the background Joe could see Red Rocks Park. It was composed of gigantic monoliths that looked like ancient, landlocked ships, sandy red and eroded.

Just looking at them Joe knew they were old.

But the display told him they were part of the Ancestral Rockies, the first mountains in the area. And they had been formed three hundred million years ago!

Joe shook his head and returned to the highway, which wound through the foothills, gaining altitude quickly. The car began to lose momentum, and Joe had to move to the slow lane as more powerful cars whizzed by.

As he traveled farther and farther into the high country, the car radio picked up more and more static, eventually losing the local stations altogether. Joe shrugged. Guess the signals can't penetrate these hills, he thought.

Ahead of him, he saw a tourist shop shaped like an Indian tepee. Joe pulled off the highway, deciding to get a snack.

After he walked past shelves of Indian pottery and jewelry, candy bars and peanuts, polished rocks and souvenirs, Joe came to a rack of postcards.

A grin lit up his face. I'll send one to Frank, he decided. A little reminder of who's stuck at home in Bayport and who's in the Rockies.

Joe looked through the postcards, staring at one that had a strange-looking creature on it. It had the body and head of a jackrabbit but the antlers of an antelope. He turned the card over and read the inscription.

"The jackalope is a very shy animal found in the high mountains. Hunters covet its beautiful

11

antlers, but the jackalope hops so quickly that it is nearly impossible to trap.''

''Sell you that, son?''

Joe looked up to see an older man wearing a cowboy hat and western shirt grinning at him— obviously, the owner of the shop.

Joe grinned back. ''Nice piece of trick photography on this card,'' he said. ''Did you ever see one of these?''

The shop owner broke into laughter. ''Well, most flatlanders, knowing no better, swear that they've seen jackalopes crossing the highway.''

''Maybe I'll send this to my brother Frank,'' Joe said.

''Hold on—you may find a better card. We have lots of strange critters running around.'' The owner chuckled again.

Joe checked out some more postcards and found a whole weird menagerie. One card touted the ''Rocky Mountain Furry Trout,'' a thick-haired fish that survived in the coldest mountain lakes. Another told about the ''Gargantuan Grasshopper,'' which was larger than the two humans posed beside it. Colorado's a strange place, Joe concluded.

He bought the postcard of the jackalope and a stamp. On the back of the card he wrote:

Dear Frank,
    Having the best time ever! Wish you were here! The sights are beautiful, and the girls

love to party! How are things at home? Having a good time with Dad and Mom?

> Your brother,
> Joe

"The postman is outside," the owner told Joe. "Catch him now, and that card will be on a plane tonight."

"Thanks." Sure enough, Joe found a postman emptying a mailbox near the road and handed him the postcard.

Although there were a few hours of light left, the sun had already set behind the western hills. Joe quickly paid for a cold drink and some snacks, then returned to the car.

Through a tunnel, around a hairpin curve, and Joe glimpsed the real mountains. Bluish, tree-bare summits rising some fourteen thousand feet above sea level filled the horizon.

Joe drove on, but as the sky continued to darken, the scenery faded into shadow. Joe had to concentrate on his driving. The road had become steep and curvy and ran along the edge of a ravine. On his left was a slope of loose boulders and rock. On his right a river roared through a mountain valley. The sound of the rushing water filled the air.

After coming out of a curve in the late twilight, Joe was heading down a deserted stretch of road. In the hazy, dark distance, something—one of those strange picture-postcard animals?—was standing in the middle of the road.

As Joe drew closer, the figure bounded directly into the path of his car. It was a man! Joe had to slam on the brakes and swerve to avoid hitting him.

He brought the car to a stop and jumped out, asking the man if he was all right.

The elderly-looking man had a hat pulled down low on his head with just a fringe of red hair hanging below. He was getting to his feet, dusting himself off.

"I'm okay, sonny," the man called as Joe walked back to him. "But my car is having a problem. I have a flat tire."

"I didn't even see you until the last possible moment," Joe said.

"No need to explain," the man said. "I'm just glad that someone was on this road. Thought I might have to spend the night out here by myself. You don't know what may happen in the wilderness once the sun goes down."

"Well, let me help you," Joe said, following the man to the edge of the road to where an old car was parked.

Joe walked around the vehicle. Its front left tire was flat.

"Problem is, I can't find my jack," the man explained.

"Hard to change a tire without one," Joe said

with a grin. "I bet there's one in my car. Wait here. I'll be right back."

Joe headed back to the rental car, took the keys from the ignition and opened the trunk. He pulled aside the spare tire and found a jack, which he began to loosen from its mount.

Then he heard a soft sound behind him—a foot scraping on the road surface. Joe started to turn, to tell the old man that he'd found the jack.

That's when he saw the tire iron swinging at his head.

Joe tried to spin away, but he was just a second too late. There was an explosion of light behind his eyes as the metal hit his skull. Then everything went black.

Everything was still dark when Joe came around—dark and stuffy. He had no idea where he was or how long he'd been unconscious. Gingerly, he touched the back of his head. He winced as his fingers probed a large welt—swollen, tender, and wet. He was probably bleeding.

After a moment, as his eyes adjusted to the darkness, he realized that he was in the trunk of a car. A tire lay beside him, and the jack ground into his back. It had to be the jack he was just removing. He was in the trunk of his own car! He tried pushing against the hood, then pounding on it. "Of all the times to get nailed," he muttered.

Joe tried to twist his body so he could push the lid with both legs, but he was too groggy to make much of an effort.

"Hey!" he shouted.

He waited for a response, but heard only the wind rustling through pine trees and the sound of the river roaring below.

"Hey!"

He rested for a moment, trying to gather his strength. Then he heard something stirring outside.

With renewed effort, Joe pounded on the lid. "Open up!" he yelled. "In the trunk!" He kicked at the metal.

He stopped, waiting for a response. Instead, he heard footsteps move away, toward the front of the car. He felt the car shift slightly as someone climbed into it. Then, after a moment, the weight shifted again, as whoever it was got out.

"Hey! Back here!"

Suddenly the car moved. The brakes were off! Someone was pushing the car from the front!

"Stop it! I'm trapped back here!"

Slowly at first, the car slid backward. Then, gaining momentum, it moved faster.

Joe could hear the pavement under the car and knew when it hit gravel. Then he heard the car brush through weeds and bounce over rocks. The roar of the river became louder. He was heading for the lip of the ravine!

He started fighting with all his strength to open the trunk. But the hood didn't budge.

Then the car tipped as the rear wheels rolled

free of the ground. Joe was thrown against the hood as the car teetered. . . .

"No! No!" he yelled.

Joe bounced around helplessly in the trunk as the car tumbled down the slopes of the canyon. He heard the windshield shatter, and a crunch of metal as the roof caved in.

Then the car backed into something large, springing the trunk lock. The lid swung up as the car bounced off a huge rock and flew high into the air. Joe had a look at where he was heading—into the boulder-strewn river of roaring white water!

Chapter

3

"ANY WORD YET?" Frank Hardy couldn't keep the anxiety out of his voice. "Has Joe called?"

His mother shook her head. "No word. This isn't like Joe. It's been two whole days."

"Where's Dad?" Frank asked, sitting down at the kitchen table in their Bayport home.

"Notifying the authorities of Joe's disappearance." Laura Hardy stared at her son for a long moment. "Frank, what's going on?"

Frank avoided her eyes. "Where's Aunt Gertrude?"

"Don't change the subject. I'm worried about Joe." Laura Hardy said sharply. She sighed and rubbed the back of her neck. "I'm sorry, Frank. I guess we're all wound up a bit too tight over this."

"It's all right, Mom," Frank said. "I'm wor-

19

ried about Joe, too." He reached across the table and took an apple from a bowl of fruit. But he wasn't really hungry. "I think I'll go for a run," he finally said.

The morning air was salty as Frank ran along the beach of Barmet Bay. Most mornings, before breakfast, Frank and Joe would run together to the beach and back. And, most mornings, Joe won.

Frank hated to admit it, but it drove him crazy. He spent his mornings exercising, doing weight training and karate workouts. Joe rolled out of bed an hour after him, and did nothing but play a little football or baseball. He was as good an athlete—or better—than Frank.

Joe jokingly referred to Frank as the brains of their operation and himself as the brawn. He was slightly shorter than Frank but stockier and more muscular. They made an excellent team. Frank sometimes wondered if the underlying competition between them was what made their team so successful.

Frank smiled, pushing himself to run faster. No, that wasn't it. They worked together so well because their abilities meshed perfectly. Because they were brothers. He'd hate to see what would happen if they ever found themselves on opposite sides.

Just as Frank returned home from his run,

Fenton Hardy walked into the kitchen, where his wife was sipping coffee.

Frank poured himself a glass of juice and joined his parents at the table.

"Is there any news?" Laura finally asked.

Fenton Hardy shook his head.

Laura Hardy shrank in her chair. "In that case, I think I'll go for a walk. I could use a little fresh air, too," she told Frank.

Frank waited for his mother to leave before he asked his father, "Nothing at all?"

"No word from Joe," Fenton said. "And no word about the hit man, either." At a look from Frank, Fenton added, "I'm doing everything I can."

Frank gripped the edge of the table, trying to stay calm. "I should have gone with Joe. It wasn't a good idea to send him alone."

Fenton Hardy shook his head. "Two people traveling together might have attracted attention. We agreed on that. And Joe won the draw to go," Fenton reminded Frank. "If we're going to play might-have-been, *I* should have gone."

"Come on, Dad. Any hood would be sure to know you. They'd follow you straight to the witness. That's why it had to be either Joe or me." He shook his head. "Joe is just too hot-headed. If he got himself into something . . ."

Fenton's eyes drifted toward the phone. "I hope not, Frank. The hoods on this case are very dangerous. Organized crime types."

"Are we going to sit here and do nothing?" Frank asked.

"I'll be in my study," Fenton said, abruptly rising to his feet. "Leave the phone line open, in case Joe calls."

The next hours were the longest in Frank's life. The kitchen phone never rang. All day Fenton shut himself up in his study. Frank could hear him talking over the private line, phone call after phone call. Laura Hardy came home and disappeared upstairs. Frank tried watching TV, then listening to music, but he couldn't get his mind off Joe.

When Fenton didn't show up for supper, Frank went to his study and knocked on the door. "I'm going after Joe," he told his father.

"I'm not sending another son out," Fenton Hardy told him firmly.

"Come on, Dad," Frank begged. "The only word we received today was some silly postcard that Joe sent two days ago! Besides, someone still has to deliver the warning to the witness."

The door opened. Fenton Hardy stared at his son. "I don't like your idea one bit," he said quietly. "But I will think about it." With that, he disappeared back into his study.

"Well, I'm not hanging around here," Frank said to himself.

He drove his van around aimlessly, up and down the streets of Bayport. All he wanted to do was help Joe. But he had to respect his father's wishes. At a train crossing, the barriers came down, lights flashing, bells clanging. Frank braked and watched the New York City express barrel past on the tracks. At least it was going someplace! He slammed the steering wheel in frustration. I'm beginning to act just like Joe, he thought.

As he was driving past the mall, Frank saw Callie Shaw, Chet Morton, and Liz Webling leaving the movies. Frank pulled up and waved to them.

"What do you say we go over to Mr. Pizza?" Chet suggested. "I'm feeling a little hungry."

"You're *always* hungry," Callie kidded him.

"That's how I maintain my figure." Chet chuckled, grabbing his middle. "Hey, Frank, why don't you come along?"

Frank shook his head. "Actually, I was hoping to take Callie away from all this."

Liz grinned and took Chet's arm. "I can take a hint," she said. "Come on, pal, lead me to that pizza."

Callie climbed in, and the van took off. The breeze from the window ruffled her blond hair as she looked at Frank. "Something's bothering you. What is it?" she asked.

Frank told her about Joe. "I want to go after him," he said.

"Sounds dangerous." Callie frowned. "Besides, you don't know for sure what happened to Joe. Maybe he's out of touch to *avoid* trouble.

You should have an idea of what you'll be fighting before you jump in the middle of it."

"I guess you're right," Frank said, reaching over to squeeze her hand.

She shuddered a little. "I always get a bad feeling in this place." She looked out across the parking lot. "It's where your car blew up—with Iola." Her voice was very quiet. "I hope Joe's all right."

Frank sat quietly for a moment, his face set. I can't stand by and do nothing, he decided.

Callie was studying him. "Frank? Are you okay?" she asked quietly. But lost in his troubled thoughts, Frank didn't answer.

It was like a nightmare playing over and over in his mind. Joe saw himself trapped in the car trunk, tumbling down the canyon wall again and again. He tried to open his eyes to stop the dreaming, but he couldn't. No, he could do nothing but live through the confusion and fear again and again.

How long ago had it *actually* happened? It could have been hours, days, or weeks. Joe had lost all notion of time. All he remembered was trying frantically to get out of the open trunk as the car tumbled toward the river. He was right above the gas tank. If it hit a boulder and exploded, he'd be splattered all over the landscape.

He'd made one desperate jump, hitting his shoulder as the lid swung closed. But he'd gotten free of the car, even if he plummeted down the slope helplessly. The last thing he saw was the blunt edge of a boulder, flying up to meet him. He twisted desperately in midair, but all that followed was this dark trance.

He had clawed his way back to consciousness. Sharp, piercing pain held him paralyzed. His body and limbs were bruised and bloody. His head throbbed in time with his heartbeat. Instinct alone got him to his feet and forced him to hobble away. Whoever had pushed him down would come to check the accident site—and maybe finish the job.

Staggering drunkenly, Joe forced his battered body along the riverbank. Stopping by a still pool of water, he looked at his reflection. It looked like something out of a splatter movie. A deep cut in his scalp had left a mask of blood over half his face, making it completely unrecognizable.

He stared at the frightening stranger in the water, then stumbled on. The river flattened and slowed. Joe stopped. Maybe he could enter the water. Perhaps its coolness would soothe his aching hurts. Moving like an old man, he gingerly climbed over some boulders lining the shore. Then he heard something duck underwater.

Leaning against a boulder, Joe blinked, trying to focus his eyes. Concentric ripples in the water marked the spot where whatever it was had disappeared. Would it surface again?

It did—and Joe gasped in amazement as a

human head broke through the water, tossing long, water-soaked hair over tanned shoulders. A girl, and a pretty one! Then she saw him and crouched in the water up to her chin!

Reeling forward, he stretched his hands toward the girl.

She reacted as if he were the star of a horror movie, moving quickly to grab for a towel lying on a boulder. Covering herself with the cloth, she climbed out of the water.

"Please," Joe tried to say, but it just came out as a moan. Then a golden retriever, teeth bared, came splashing through the water, snarling at him.

Joe tried to pull himself together, to defend himself, but everything was swirling around him. He looked at the girl and heard a voice—his own? hers?—whispering, "Help me!"

Then he collapsed, helplessly crumpling into darkness.

Chapter

4

"CAN YOU TELL me anything more? Please try to remember," Frank Hardy said. "It's really important." He leaned across the rental car counter at Stapleton Airport. In his hand was his one slim lead to Joe, the jackalope postcard which Joe had sent him.

The clerk, a young woman with a stiff blond hairdo, thought for a moment, then said, "I'm sorry. There's a few conventions in town, plus the usual tourists. I showed you our records, so you know what kind of car he rented. But I just don't remember anything else about him."

"He may have asked directions to the mountains. Does that help?" Frank asked.

"I just can't remember your brother," the clerk said. "I mean, I remember helping someone who looks like that picture you showed me. But that was a few days ago. If he was headed for the mountains, you've got a big job ahead of you."

Frank glanced over the clerk's shoulder. On the wall was tacked a road map of Colorado and the surrounding states. And the mountains filled an enormous part of the map. If Joe were lost up there, it would take a miracle to find him, Frank thought to himself. But he knew the route Joe was supposed to follow, and now he knew what Joe was driving. That was a start.

It had taken some doing to convince his father to let him try this mission—they had argued well into the night. Finally, as much because of exhaustion as discussion, Fenton Hardy agreed to let Frank go. If they waited much longer, Joe's trail might be too cold to follow.

"We can only hope Joe's alive," Fenton finally said. "And you'll have to find our witness—and that hit man."

Frank barely had time to pack a bag before his father was hurrying him to the airport.

"I'm giving you twenty-four hours," Fenton had warned Frank. "If there's no sign of Joe or the hit man, I want you home. Understand?"

"Okay, Dad." Frank looked up at his father's pale, drawn face. "Everything will turn out all right. I promise."

The rental car clerk's voice cut through his thoughts. "Sorry I couldn't be of more help. Good luck in finding your brother."

"Thanks, anyway," Frank said, flipping the

postcard against his palm. Suddenly an idea came to him.

"Can I bother you one more second?" he said to the clerk.

"No bother."

"Have you ever seen one of these?" Frank asked, showing her the postcard.

The clerk studied the postcard, then grinned. "Well, it's not too easy to see a jackalope—since it doesn't exist. It's only a gag postcard, understand. Tourists buy them by the gross."

"Where are they sold?" Frank asked.

"All over the state," the clerk said. "May I see it?"

"There's no clue on it," Frank said. "Just a joke message from Joe."

"But there's also a postmark," said the clerk. "Maybe I'll recognize where it's from."

Frank handed over the postcard, and she examined the inky postmark which had cancelled the stamp. "Summit County," she said. "I know where that is. Up in the mountains, about sixty miles due west of here. And I bet that I know exactly where your brother bought this."

"Really? Where?"

"There's a tourist shop right off the highway. It's built to look like an Indian tent. The owner loves this sort of junk."

Frank took back the postcard. "Thanks. At least it's a start."

In a rental car of his own, Frank began to trace

29

Joe's tracks from the Denver airport. On the highway, heading west, Frank turned on the radio. It was too much to hope for news about Joe, but he wanted a weather report. Already his mind was working, trying to estimate the driving time to the mountains, taking into consideration the weather and amount of traffic.

Most of the time these mental exercises were just games. Frank knew this, but he tried to keep his mind sharp with constant practice.

At first Frank felt confident that he could find Joe. Call it a hunch, but it would not be the first time that Frank got his younger brother out of a tight spot. All too often, Joe's hot head got him into trouble, charging into situations without thinking things through. *Caution* was not to be found in Joe Hardy's vocabulary.

Frank smiled to himself. What dumb thing had Joe done this time? Run out of gas on a deserted mountain road? Completed his mission and then run into a few girls, forgetting altogether to call home?

The car began to lose its momentum as the incline of the road became steeper. Frank hit the accelerator, wanting to maintain a speed just below the legal limit. Ahead he saw the Rocky Mountains. Massive, imposing, endless. And Frank's optimism began to fade.

How could one person search a whole mountain range? he asked himself. It could take weeks, even months, to track Joe down. He could already be dead—or dying—before Frank reached the foothills.

Still, he couldn't turn back.

Joe, sweaty, breathing heavily, fought against delirium. His mind, like some video machine gone berserk, kept flashing brief, violent scenes —confused memories. Voices, momentary images of faces and scenes turned over and over. The people and places were both incredibly familiar and frighteningly alien.

Tumbling in and out of darkness, Joe found himself struggling again with Al-Rousasa, the terrorist who had killed Iola Morton.

He and Joe were fighting again not far from where Iola had been murdered.

"Wait a second, this has to be a dream," Joe told himself. "This can't be happening again. Or is it happening for the very first time?"

Joe didn't have any more time to wonder. Al-Rousasa hurled him against a concrete bench. The impact left Joe seeing stars as the terrorist knelt over him, raising his knife for the kill. Joe, cut and bleeding, got off a perfect roundhouse right straight into Al-Rousasa's face.

The punch knocked the terrorist backward and over a safety rail, where he could drop sixty feet to the mall below. But no. Al-Rousasa had the agility of a cat. He twisted himself around in midair, snatching at the rail and catching onto the edge of the floor.

Joe stood, glaring down at those white-knuckled hands and the dark eyes burning with hatred. A quick stomp on those hands, a kick into that despised face, and Iola's killer would be gone. . . .

Suddenly the dream shifted, and the terrorist dissolved into a cloud of fog. Out of the haze appeared the laughing face of a beautiful girl with pixielike features.

"Iola!" Joe heard himself call. "Iola, please forgive me!"

She turned and ran away. Joe tried to follow, but it was as if his feet were fixed in concrete. "Iola! Wait."

Suddenly Joe felt himself swept up. He was swooping along a cliff, flying over sharp-edged rocks. He could feel the wind whipping past him, blowing the mane against his face—the mane? Now he was on a horse, galloping madly.

Joe gripped the horse tightly with his knees and with his arms wrapped around the animal's neck. Then the gunshots came streaking past.

The horse raced across a pasture, then down a moonlit asphalt road. Hoofbeats thundered so loudly that Joe had to yell to make himself heard.

"We've done it! We've shaken them!" he shouted triumphantly, looking over his shoulder—at what? Where were the others?

Only an empty highway stretched behind him.

He faced front again, to see a huge mountain of a man preparing to shoot a girl. The girl charged him, moving without a word, a knife held tightly in her hand. She would never reach the man in time. "No!" Joe screamed, but he was too late.

The Super Blackhawk came up, fired. The bullet caught the girl in the chest, whipping her about violently. She hit the ground and lay motionless.

Not caring if the guy shot him, too, Joe jumped for him. But the man dissolved, and Joe found himself landing on hard concrete.

"Joe!"

He scrambled to his knees, to find Iola standing where the girl had gone down. She was surrounded by flames, and calling his name.

"You've got to save me, Joe! You can't let me die!"

Joe hurled himself forward, but never made it to that ring of fire. Someone was in his way—a tall, dark-haired guy about his own age. He looked so familiar, but Joe didn't recognize him.

But that didn't matter then. Joe tried to shove his way past him, to get to Iola. But the dark stranger didn't move. He held Joe back.

The next thing Joe knew, he was throwing a punch. It didn't land. The dark-haired stranger ducked. But when Joe tried to dart past again, the stranger grabbed him.

It was like wrestling with an octopus. Joe couldn't get loose. And all the time he fought, he could hear Iola in the background, screaming.

He looked into his captor's face, and the

stranger began laughing. Sometimes it sounded as if he were just kidding. Other times his laughter was mocking—threatening.

The laughter became louder and louder, mingling with and drowning out Iola's screams. Then Joe was screaming, too. "Iola! It's not my fault! Stop it. *Stop it!*"

His body arched with pain as someone shook him violently. Then he realized his swollen eyes were open. This was no dream!

Squinting, he couldn't make out who was looming over him. Was it a friend or enemy? Was it the dark-haired stranger?

Still groggy, he struck out and his hand clamped around a neck. He heard a gasp as the stranger fell to the floor.

"I'll get you!" Joe screamed. "I'll kill you with my bare hands!"

Chapter

5

FRANK'S SHOULDERS SLUMPED in defeat. For hours, well into a long, long night, he had searched for Joe. But there wasn't even one solid clue as to where Joe was. Joe had started off on the route his father had given him, and then it seemed as if he had disappeared.

The owner of the tepee tourist shop had remembered Joe, but he had provided no concrete leads.

"Sorry," he'd said. "I can't keep track of every lowlander coming this way. Sure I can't interest you in a nice silver bracelet for your girlfriend?"

"Girlfriend? What makes you think I have a girlfriend?"

That got a chuckle from the owner. "Fella like you would be sure to have a girlfriend."

All Frank had wanted was a phone. He had called back to Bayport from the shop. His parents had nothing to report. But Fenton Hardy had reminded him that his twenty-four hours would be up the next afternoon.

Frank had answered that he wasn't going to leave Colorado without some information about Joe's fate.

After leaving the tourist shop, Frank had covered the main roads of Summit County until well past sundown. He'd stopped at gas stations and truck stops, at restaurants and motels, describing Joe's car, showing Joe's photo. He had talked with the local law, asking if anything unusual—an accident, a rock slide, a shooting—had been reported. He checked with the local hospitals. But everywhere he went, Frank had come up empty.

Finally, he couldn't drive any farther and pulled into a rest area. Under better circumstances the place would have been very restful. It was off the main road and had several picnic tables surrounded by tall, thin pines and aspens. Nearby, a stream ran downhill through a canyon.

But Frank found little rest. When his eyes closed, all he could envision were horrible scenes. Joe hurt and lost. Joe attacked by the very hit man he was trying to stop. Joe dazed and wandering. Joe . . . Joe . . . Joe . . .

Frank napped for a little while, then shook himself awake, his eyes and mouth feeling gummy. He started the car and looked for a place to eat.

Now he was sitting in a truck stop. It was late, closer to sunrise than midnight. The only other customers, truck drivers.

Frank sat at the counter, sipping a large glass of soda, barely touching the hamburger and fries in front of him. His place mat was a map of Colorado, the kind with facts about tourist attractions.

Frank pushed his food away and unfolded a road map. With a pen he marked the places he had already visited.

"Looking for a place to bed down for the night?" the waitress asked. "There's a decent motel about three miles down the road."

"No," Frank told her. "I've got to keep moving. May I have my check, please?"

The waitress totaled up Frank's bill and left it on the counter. "You look pretty tired," she said. "I hope that you're not planning to do much more driving. The roads around here can be dangerous in the dark."

Frank put some money on the counter. He shook his head, trying to come up with a new course of action. The waitress marched over to freshen the coffee for two truckers sharing a booth.

"How are you guys tonight?" she asked.

"Stuck here," one trucker said with a grin.

"How about two slices of your famous apple pie?"

"And keep the coffee coming," said the other trucker. "Might as well stay put till they get that accident cleaned up."

"Accident?" the waitress asked.

"Heard it over my CB," he said. "Road's closed up near Cripple Mine. They found some car went off the road, and they've closed it till a tow truck can pull the car up from the river. Decided to do it now, so they wouldn't block the road during the day."

Frank spun around on his stool, giving the truckers his full attention.

"Was it a bad crash?" the waitress asked.

"Yeah. But they think it happened a while ago. Some guy just reported it today, though. A buddy of mine was the last truck they let through. He was passing by just after the police had arrived. Told me about it over the CB. Strangest thing, he said the car had been picked clean of any ID. The glove compartment was stripped. No registration. Even the license plates were missing."

"Well, who was driving?" the waitress asked.

"No sign of anyone." The trucker shrugged. "I can't figure it."

The truckers and waitress continued to talk, but Frank turned back to the road map before him.

"Cripple Mine," he whispered to himself, tracing over his map. His finger had strayed across the border into Utah before he shook his head, realizing he was too tired to use common sense.

He turned the map around to check the directory of places listed on the back. Sure enough, there was a Cripple Mine.

Using the location code, Frank first circled the general area, then, peering closer he zeroed in on Cripple Mine. He circled it with a pen. Using the mileage legend he figured that he could reach Cripple Mine by sunrise.

Frank quietly folded the map and left. He was feeling some hope, even though that accident sounded bad. What if he finally found Joe's car, only to learn that something horrible had happened to his brother?

Joe Hardy had tumbled to the floor, a cold grip around his enemy's throat. Hands were feebly beating against his wrists, but they couldn't break his hold. The dark-haired stranger wasn't so strong now! He'd kill him!

He stared at his enemy—and leapt back, blinking. "Am I dreaming?" he whispered to himself. The stranger had disappeared. Instead, his hands were locked on the throat of an auburn-haired girl with lovely green eyes—apprehensive eyes at that moment, as she huddled on the floor, arms raised to protect herself.

He reached up and felt a bandage wrapped around his head. "Wha-what's going on?" he asked, his voice thin and reedy.

"You began shouting and tossing around on the bed," the girl said. "I tried to shake you awake—and you started strangling me!" She looked at him nervously. "Do you always wake up like that?"

Joe leaned back against the bed, his head spinning. Little by little, he took in his surroundings. A rustic cabin with log walls. A small, single room equipped with a wooden table and chairs, one bed and several folding cots, and a cast iron wood-burning stove.

"I'm sorry if I scared you," he finally said.

The girl dropped her defensive pose. "You could make a career out of scaring people—like when you came up to the river."

Joe rubbed his head. "You—you were the girl in the water!"

Her face went red. "I was—um—skinny-dipping, and then you came lurching out of the rocks at me like some kind of monster. My dog, Lucky, ran at you—he's a good watchdog. I thought he'd have to attack you. But you just fell on your face."

The girl helped Joe back onto the bed. "I could see that you were pretty badly banged up, especially when I couldn't revive you. I heard later about a car half-buried in the river. Was that yours?"

For an instant Joe remembered tumbling through the air. "Yeah," he muttered.

"You were lucky you survived." Joe nodded.

"Anyway, I dragged you back here. It took a while, because you were bleeding pretty badly, and you weighed a ton! I was afraid you wouldn't make it." She smiled sweetly and began readjusting Joe's bandage.

"Once I got you here," she continued, "my Uncle Delbert helped me get you into bed and worked on your wounds. We didn't dare move you. The closest hospital is miles and miles away."

"I owe you and your uncle a lot," Joe said. "Thanks."

The girl smiled at him. "My name is Rita, by the way. My uncle's not here right now. He went out for, uh, supplies."

"I don't know how I can thank you." Joe tried to sit up. Pain brought his hands to his temples and forehead.

"You kept muttering in your sleep. I thought that maybe we should take our chances and move you to a hospital—even with the long drive."

"Long drive? We must really be isolated," Joe said.

Rita nodded. "Uncle Delbert likes the quiet." She dampened a cloth and lightly ran it over Joe's face. "You're looking a lot better. How do you feel?"

"Like I was hit with a ton of bricks," Joe said. He attempted a smile, but a sudden pain in his head made him groan instead.

"Well, you'll need a lot more rest. Your body

will need time to heal,'' Rita said. She collected the cloth and bowl of water and began to move away. "You know," she said, stopping, "you haven't told me your name."

"I'm—I'm—" Joe began to say, expecting his name to naturally follow. He rubbed his head. "I can't remember!"

"What?" Rita said. "Are you joking?"

"I can't remember!" Joe rose up in panic.

"Now, lie back and try to rest. Remember, you took an awful thump on the head." She covered him with a quilt and then pulled a chair beside the bed and held his hand. "Just take it easy," she said. "Don't try to force anything. It'll all come back to you."

"I can't remember my own name!" Joe began to push himself off the bed.

Rita gently pushed him back. "Where do you think you're going? You can't travel."

"You don't understand," Joe's voice rose. "There's something I have to do!"

"What's that?" Rita asked.

"I—can't remember!" Joe said.

"Then you can't do it, can you?" Rita said, trying to calm him. "First you have to remember your name."

"But I can't!" Joe's whole body was quivering.

"Calm down!" she said gently. "I'm here to help you. Just close your eyes. Relax, and tell me what comes into your mind."

Joe closed his eyes and sank back into the soft

pillow. At first his mind was a clean slate—then a hazy image appeared. Slowly it became clearer—a girl seated in a sedan. "Iola," he whispered sadly.

"Iola?" Rita said. "That's an interesting name. Is that the name of your hometown or something?"

"No, no. It's the name of a girl," he said.

"Your sister?" Rita asked. "Your girlfriend, perhaps?"

Then he saw the flames, and the dark stranger's face, just like in his dream. "Iola, I-I've got to help her," Joe stammered. "He's stopping me!"

"He?" Rita echoed. "Who is 'he'?"

"There's danger. Awful danger!" Joe opened his eyes and sat up. "Something evil is outside."

"Please, please calm down," Rita said. "That's only the wind moving through the trees. Believe me, we're miles from the nearest neighbors."

"No!" Joe told her. "You've got to believe me. It's lurking outside, ready to hurt us!" He lurched up from the bed and stumbled to the door, pulling on the handle.

The heavy wooden door swung open—to reveal a man standing on the porch, a rifle in his hands.

"Hold it right there, buddy," the man said. "You make a move and I'll use this thing!"

Chapter

6

FRANK HARDY DROVE frantically through the Rocky Mountain dawn. Sunlight was a long time coming to the low canyons where his route took him. The sun had been up for an hour before it was high enough in the sky to climb over the craggy mountaintops.

Till then, Frank had driven through a faint glow. Little by little, though, the glow increased, bringing a pink tone to the rocks around him. Then, as more light hit the rocks, the pink intensified into reddish brown.

The air began to warm, and Frank realized he no longer needed the car heater. He turned it off and opened a window. Cool, dry breezes filled the car, bringing with them a scent of pine.

It was a beautiful spectacle—but Frank hardly noticed. Except for a brief nap, he had been up all night. His whole body ached from lack of sleep. His stomach rumbled, his neck and back were shot through with pain. His mind buzzed with a series of unanswerable "what ifs."

"What if I can't locate Cripple Mine?"

"What if the cops don't let me through?"

"What if the car's already been towed away?"

"What if I'm forced to return to Bayport without Joe?"

"What if I find Joe dead?"

"What if the hit man is lying in wait for *me*?" The road passed through some woods. For just a moment Frank thought about stopping the car, walking through the woods, kneeling beside a brook, and rubbing some of its icy water over his tired face. But he drove on.

"Hang on, Joe," Frank whispered. "I'm coming. I'm coming, brother."

He curved around a bend in the highway to find a patrolman removing a wooden barricade, to open the road to traffic again.

Frank slowed, checking out the scene. Through the open window he heard the roar of a raging river. Beside him he saw the steel guardrail smashed apart, with tire tracks rolling off the road's edge and disappearing into the ravine.

Just ahead of this, parked at the side of the ravine, were a tow truck carrying a wreck and a highway patrol car. An officer was jotting notes down, while the tow truck operator waited.

Frank stopped and shouted out the window, "Excuse me. Is this near Cripple Mine?"

"Yes, it is. But just keep moving, son," the officer said. "Got to keep the road clear."

"Looks like some accident," Frank said. "How did the guy who was driving come out?"

"We found nothing but the wreck itself," the officer said. "No body, no identification."

"Well, thank you," Frank said. He accelerated slightly, moving past the tow truck.

He nearly slammed to a stop as he studied the wrecked car—the same make and model that Joe had rented. "No one could have survived in that," he whispered to himself. The windshield and all the windows of the car had been shattered. The roof was flattened against the body. The engine was in the backseat. The sides had been punched in like a collapsed milk carton.

Frank's face was grim as he drove away. If Joe had been in there . . .

He drove a mile or so, then finding a place to pull off, he hid his car among some trees. Then he walked back along the road toward the accident site.

Seeing the approaching roof lights of the tow truck and patrol car, Frank ducked for cover. He crouched low in some bushes while the procession passed by. Then he jogged along the asphalt road.

He followed the guardrail until its violent break. Glancing down the rocky ravine Frank

47

could see the tracks the wreck had made as it was winched up from the river. Gingerly Frank stepped off the edge and started down the ravine.

He picked his way carefully. One false step and he'd be unable to regain his balance. He'd tumble out of control over sharp boulders to the wild river below. He leaned into the hill, until he reached the bottom.

The sun was high over the pines now. It gave perfect light for Frank's search. His eyes focused on the ground, looking for anything the highway patrol might have missed.

Paint on some boulders and a deep indentation at the river's edge indicated to Frank where the wreck had landed. He remembered how the wreck had looked. About the only part of the car not severely damaged had been the trunk. Maybe, if Joe had survived, he might have gotten out through there.

Moving farther downstream Frank spied a tire iron among some rocks. It couldn't have been there long—no cobwebs, moss, or rust. Frank picked up the steel bar and inspected it closely. Near the top he found what looked like a cluster of hairs glued to the iron with dried blood.

The muscles in Frank's jaw tensed as he took this in. The crash looked very little like an accident now. Whoever had stripped the car had a purpose—a deadly one.

Hefting the tire iron like a club, Frank moved on. He stopped to examine a flat boulder—and the sticky, reddish stain on it. A smear of dry blood, as if someone had stopped to rest—or die.

Frank looked downstream. Someone could have followed a narrow trail up the rocky slope toward the trees. Or, someone could have walked along the rocks lining the river edge.

But, Frank deduced, if someone was injured and bleeding, he would follow the river trail, since it would be easier.

So Frank began to follow the river. His tiredness fell away from him now; every sense was awake and alert. He cast back and forth over the soft mud, finding one print and then another. The pattern they made looked like a drunken—or injured—stumble. Then a new set of prints were introduced—not human. Frank knelt to examine them. They looked like the prints of a large dog.

Frank continued on and spied a new set of human prints. Small bare footprints, most likely a woman's or boy's. And, off to the side, caught in some brambles, was a white bath towel!

Climbing onto a boulder, Frank tried to get an aerial view of the three sets of prints. Yes, it all made sense. It looked as if the small prints had come from the water. Then whoever made those prints dragged the person who made the larger prints away. The larger person was probably injured. Frank crossed his fingers and barely allowed himself to hope it was Joe.

But who were they for sure? And where did they go?

Frank followed the prints until he was confronted by a massive boulder blocking the river path. The ground all around it was rocky, and the prints disappeared.

"Just my luck," Frank said. He ran across the rocky ground, which led to the edge of some woods. Casting around, Frank inspected the area, looking for any sign—a broken branch or scuffed pine needles—anything that would indicate that somebody had been dragged that way.

For the first time he felt a faint glimmer of hope. Perhaps Joe had survived the wreck and somehow had found help. Maybe Frank could find him.

But one disturbing question remained. Who had used the bloody tire iron? And if he used it once against Joe, would he be satisfied that he had done his job? Or would he try to kill Joe again?

Chapter
7

JOE WAS VERY much alive and trying to stay that way. "Now, hold on, mister," he said taking a step forward.

"No, *you* hold on," said the man, thrusting his rifle at Joe. "I've got a lot of questions I want answered." The rifle was pointed straight at Joe's chest.

"Anything you say," Joe said soothingly. He managed another step forward, then swung his arm quickly, batting the rifle aside. After a quick scuffle, he had the weapon in his hands, a little amazed that he had won in his weakened condition.

But the man before him was even more feeble. He could have been anywhere between forty and fifty. But he looked wasted. His face and neck were gaunt. His skin had a pale, pasty quality, and his eyes showed both fear and sleeplessness.

"Go ahead," the man said, his face stony. "Shoot me. End it!"

But Rita screamed. "Don't! It's my uncle!"

Joe glanced from the man to Rita, then lowered the weapon. "Do you always carry a rifle when you go out for supplies?" he asked suspiciously.

"Uncle Delbert and I are down here for a hunting trip," Rita explained. "We're from Wyoming."

"Right," Delbert said. "Whenever I go out, I carry the gun. I might get a lucky shot at something."

Or *someone,* Joe thought. He looked back into the cabin. Plenty of wood had been cut and was stacked near the stove. Provisions lined the kitchen shelves. These people weren't there for a simple vacation, and it didn't look as if they needed supplies.

"How long have you been here?" Joe asked.

"A couple of days," Rita said quickly.

"Shot anything?"

"Nope. All I've seen so far were a couple of jackalopes," Rita answered, smiling slightly.

"Jackalopes?" Joe echoed. An image flickered through his mind. "Knock if off, Rita. Anyone who spends time in the Rockies knows jackalopes don't exist. I sent a gag postcard with a jackalope to my brother."

"Your brother," Rita said. "Then your memory is coming back.'' Eager to change the subject, she explained about Joe's memory loss to her uncle.

Joe stood very still, trying to recall more images. A mall—a sporting goods store, where he had bought a pair of— ''My boots,'' Joe whispered. ''My hiking boots.''

Rita stared at him. ''What's that?''

''There's something hidden in one of my boots,'' Joe told her.

Uncle Delbert raised his head. ''Hidden?'' he repeated.

The three of them went back into the cabin, and Joe found his hiking boots by the door. Rita had cleaned and polished them. He picked up the right boot, feeling along the sole. Then he twisted the heel—it swung out!

Nestled inside the hollow heel was a small capsule.

Joe pulled the capsule open, and a scrap of paper dropped into his hand.

Eagerly, he unrolled the paper. He smoothed it against his palm and stared at it in frustration.

''What does it say?'' Rita asked.

''It's just a line of letters.'' Joe tried to pronounce them. '' 'On-ot-ow-at-ish-ik-a.' ''

''May I try?'' Rita asked. Joe handed her the message. '' 'O-no-to-wa-*tish*-i-ka?' Maybe it's an Indian name?''

''It's a code,'' Joe said. ''And I don't have the

key!'' He paused for a second. How had he known that?

Delbert snatched the paper from his niece's hand. ''Where did you get this?'' he demanded.

''I can't remember,'' Joe said miserably. ''I can't even read what it says!''

Delbert's face was hard and suspicious as he looked at Joe. He had just opened his mouth to say something, when frenzied snarling and barking rang out from outside the cabin.

''Lucky!'' Rita moved to a window.

But Delbert grabbed her arm. ''Stay low,'' he said, stretching his hand out to Joe. ''I need that rifle, youngster.''

Joe handed it over, and Delbert jacked a round into the chamber. He threw open the door and dove outside. After rolling across the porch, he came up in a crouch.

Lucky gave a yelp of pain and ran to the door.

Both Joe and Delbert scanned the area, looking along Lucky's line of flight. No one was there. Delbert backed through the door, his finger still on the trigger.

Rita was kneeling on the floor, checking Lucky. ''His whole side is sore. I think someone hit him or kicked him!''

Delbert ran from window to window, pulling the curtains tight, blocking the view from anyone watching outside. Then he sat down by the stove and looked at Joe's coded message. ''This has gone far enough,'' he said. ''You kids have to get out of here!''

Moving methodically, his senses alert and supercharged, Frank bushwhacked his way through the woods. The floor of pine needles had been disturbed, here and there, giving him a path to follow. He stopped to check out a muddy patch. Footprints—the same footprints he had seen near the river. Farther on, losing the trail again, he found some white strands caught on a branch. Clothing threads, he thought.

He continued on, but stopped when he came to a steep rocky slope. No one could drag another person up there—but which way had they gone around?

Frank decided to give ten minutes to the right-hand trail. If I don't find anything by then, I'll turn back and try the other side.

He pushed on, finding no hint of a trail. At a gap in the rocks where a small stream trickled downhill, he stopped to look for tracks. There was something in the soft mud. He leaned down for a closer look. A large animal had passed by there, its paw pads shaped like a cat's. ''Great,'' Frank muttered. ''That's all I'd need to do—meet a mountain lion.''

He turned around and slowly retraced his steps, keeping an eye out for anything he might have missed. Returning to the place where he had turned, he headed left. The way was smoother. Yes, it was the trail to try.

A few minutes on he stopped and inspected a blurred footprint. With renewed confidence, he quickened his pace, thinking that *something* must lie ahead!

In the cabin, Rita stared at her uncle. "What do you mean, you want us to get out of here!"

Delbert glanced at Joe. "I think you should get him and his message to the law as soon as possible. That means the county sheriff in Corralville."

"But that's so far away!" Rita objected.

"Then you'd best be going," Delbert said. "That message may be important."

"I'm not leaving you alone here," Rita told her uncle.

"Well, I'm not leaving the cabin empty with some prowler out there," Delbert answered. This time, both of them gave Joe a look.

Joe felt as if he'd come in at the middle of a movie. The whole conversation didn't make any sense.

Delbert dug into his pocket. "Here're the keys to the Jeep. I want both of you out of here. *Now!*"

He moved to a small pantry off the kitchen and took out a box.

"What are you doing?" Rita stared at the box.

"I just want my old things nearby," Delbert

said, setting the box on the table before him. "You two had best be going while you still can."

Rita seemed on the verge of tears. Joe walked to Delbert's Jeep, wondering what was going on.

"Do you feel well enough to drive?" Delbert asked Joe.

"Yes." Joe got behind the wheel. His head was still a bit foggy, but Rita was visibly upset and in no condition to drive.

"Stick to the main roads—Rita will give you directions," Delbert said. "You take good care of her," he added in a softer voice.

Joe was completely baffled. Until then Rita had been taking care of *him*. He started the Jeep and pulled away from the cabin. They headed up an old logging road, bumping over half-buried rocks.

When they were out of sight of the cabin, Joe stopped the Jeep and turned to Rita. "You're not from Wyoming. Right?"

"Right. We're from the East Coast. And I didn't want to come here. The idea of living out in the wilderness scared me. But I've gotten to like the quiet. The chance to see nature."

Joe was getting tired of not understanding. "Rita, what's going on here?"

Tears began to stream down her face. "I—I can't tell you."

"What's so important about that box your uncle took from the pantry?" Joe pressed.

"Please!" Fear filled her eyes.

"We're not moving until you tell me why that

57

box is so important.'' Joe stared at her, waiting for an answer.

''All right.'' Rita seemed to shrink in her seat. ''I never even knew that he'd brought that box along. But I know what he keeps inside it. A pistol—and plenty of ammunition.''

''A pistol,'' Joe repeated. Suddenly an image popped into his head. It was the dark-haired stranger from his dreams, a gun in his hands.

And two words swam up to his consciousness—*hit man!*

Joe grabbed Rita's wrist. ''Your uncle—he's afraid for his life, isn't he?''

He swung the Jeep around and headed back down toward the cabin.

''What are you doing?'' Rita demanded. ''You're going the wrong way.''

''We've got to stop him!'' Joe shouted above the roar of the Jeep.

The Jeep bounced along the road, throwing up a trail of dust. Joe held on to the steering wheel, and Rita gripped the seat beneath her.

''Stop who?'' she shouted.

The Jeep reached the clearing where the cabin stood, and Joe leapt out. The Jeep sputtered and died in its tracks. Rita jumped out and tried to stop Joe, but she couldn't catch him.

He was running flat out when a pistol shot rang out!

Chapter

8

FRANK HALTED AT the edge of a clearing and saw a cabin. He stepped back into the bushes, out of sight of any watchful eyes peering from the windows. Crawling on hands and knees, he eased forward to scout the place out. It looked deserted. No smoke rose from the stone chimney. There were no cars parked in front. The windows and the door were closed.

Frank, resting his hand on the ground as he crouched, felt something beneath his fingertips. He held up a small shred of thin paper—the kind used to wrap cigarettes. The paper was still white, so it hadn't been there very long. Frank smelled it—there was still a hint of smoke.

Someone had been watching the cabin just as he was. But the person had smoked a cigarette, then field-stripped it to hide the fact. It was dumb luck that Frank had found the paper. Why such secrecy—unless the other person was up to something unpleasant!

Frank was about to start circling the cabin when he heard a dog bark. He stayed crouched in the brush as the barking and snarling continued.

Then Frank heard a car engine and an instant later saw a Jeep roar into view and stop. Someone vaulted out and ran for the cabin. Frank squinted, trying to identify the person. Could it be Joe? No. It looked as though this guy was wearing a turban.

Frank blinked. But that made no sense. He strained for a better view. The figure was too far away for Frank to see him clearly.

Then the sound of gunshots exploded just above his head. Frank dove for cover. He had been spotted!

After staying quiet for a minute, he crept back to the edge of the clearing to a new observation site. But when he got there, the turbaned person had disappeared.

Frank waited a moment or two. Part of him wanted to throw caution aside and rush the cabin, settling this thing right away. But the person he saw didn't look exactly like Joe. And someone inside that cabin had a gun and was willing to use it. No point in taking foolish risks.

So Frank crept deep into the woods. He would eventually make his way to the cabin.

* * *

At the first pistol shot, Joe whirled and tackled Rita, dragging her to cover behind the Jeep as two more shots sounded.

"Wait here," he told her.

"No! I'm going with you," she said through gritted teeth.

"Rita, I'm just going to check out the cabin. If Delbert is all right, I'll signal for you. But if I'm not back in a few minutes, you have to take the Jeep and get the sheriff."

Rita gave him a mutinous glare but said nothing.

Joe, crouching low, faded back, and used the trees for cover as he sneaked behind the cabin. He crept up to a window, and slowly rose to his full height and peered through the glass.

Inside, Delbert appeared to be alone. Frightened and agitated, he darted back and forth at the front windows, looking out. He held the rifle in one hand and a pistol in the other. The dog stood guard near the door, barking furiously.

Delbert sure has a nervous trigger finger, Joe thought. What's he afraid of?

The words *hit man* went through his mind again.

Joe shrugged. Whatever was going on, one thing was certain. When they left, he and Rita would take Delbert with them. He was in too much danger, alone in the woods. Of course, there was still the job of getting inside to tell Delbert without getting shot.

Gingerly, Joe unwrapped the bandage around

his head, planning to wave it as a flag of truce. Then he heard Rita shouting, "Don't shoot! It's me, Rita!"

Frank, hearing the girl's voice, peered out of the brush. A young woman came running from the Jeep toward the cabin.

Then another figure came to join her from the far side of the cabin. Frank gasped. It was Joe! His younger brother looked much the worse for wear—but he was alive and apparently all right!

Frank was about to shout to him when a man waving a pistol stepped from the cabin door. Frank remained down as the man motioned Joe and the girl inside.

Still hiding, Frank tried to make sense of the situation. A cabin in the mountains, Joe hurt, a man with a gun—Wait a minute! Joe was heading for a cabin in the first place! Could it be this place?

He shut his eyes, trying to trace the route Joe was supposed to follow. Of course, that route would have followed roads. Frank had cut cross-country on foot. Without a good map, he couldn't be sure. Still, it made a reasonable theory.

But the guy with the gun? Was he the fugitive witness? Or could Joe have walked into the arms of the hit man? Frank was determined to find out as he moved deeper into the woods so he could use its cover to circle to the rear of the cabin.

* * *

Behind the log walls, Rita's Uncle Delbert shouted, "Why'd you come back?"

"Who were you shooting at?" Rita asked.

"I saw someone moving outside. At least I thought I did—now I'm not sure. No one returned my fire. Must have been my nerves making me see things."

"You don't understand," Joe cut in. "Someone *is* trying to kill you!"

Delbert seemed to sag. "I understand plenty," he said quietly, dropping into one of the kitchen chairs. Rita stepped behind him and began to rub his shoulders and neck.

"Try to relax," she told him. "It makes no sense for you to stay here. Come with us. *Please* come with us."

"I can't!" Delbert moaned. He looked up at Joe. "Why did you come back? Did you start remembering?"

Joe reached into his pocket and took out the undecipherable message. He held it out to Delbert. "Was this meant for you?"

Delbert gave him a calculating stare. "If I say yes, you'll stay and try to help me. So I'll just tell you to get it to the sheriff—along with Rita."

"I'm not leaving you," Rita insisted. "We'll see this through together." She was shaking with tears.

"No, we won't," Delbert said. "I'll end it here. See, honey, I don't have much time left for run-

63

ning, anyway. I'm terminally ill. The doctor in Corralville told me months ago. There's no hope for me.''

He picked up the box on the kitchen table and reloaded his pistol, looking totally drained. Then he slumped down in his chair, facing the door. The golden retriever came over and lay down at his feet.

''There's only one thing I want,'' Delbert said. ''And that's seeing Rita safe.'' He stared at Joe. ''I can't escape. And I'd just as soon die here. Maybe I can take out the guy who's chasing us.''

''You don't have to die,'' Joe said.

''All three of us may die if you two insist on staying here,'' Delbert said. ''Now go, and that's an order. Take the Jeep and clear out.''

''Let *him* go,'' Rita said, motioning at Joe. ''I'm staying.''

Delbert pushed himself to his feet. For a moment it looked as though he were about to lose his temper, then his expression softened. ''Rita, girl, you are my life. Please. If you won't leave because I order you, leave because I'm begging you. You must go on without me.''

Rita ran into Delbert's arms. They embraced each other fiercely—as if they knew it was their last goodbye.

After a moment Rita reluctantly pulled away. ''Come on,'' she said to Joe. ''We'd better get going.''

Delbert tried to give Joe the pistol. "Here," he said, "you may need this."

Joe shook his head.

Delbert gave him the ghost of a smile as he saw them out the door, but his face was set and pale. All he could manage was a wave of his hand as Joe led Rita from the cabin.

They got into the Jeep, threw it into first, and climbed the ridge behind the cabin. The road was steep and loaded with hairpin turns, so the cabin was in and out of view, getting smaller and smaller with every turn.

Rita, her eyes swollen and teary, stared over her shoulder at her home.

Joe wanted to console her, but didn't know what to say. Instead, he concentrated on his driving. It was so weird. How could he remember how to drive a Jeep—yet not remember his own name?

The Jeep came around a sharp hairpin turn, and, below, the cabin came back into view. It looked so peaceful down in the clearing, like something in an enchanted forest.

And then it exploded! A star of brightness appeared on one wall, and chunks of wood and stone shot high into the air. Flames blossomed in the wreckage.

As smoke and ash filled the air, Joe braked to a stop, staring in disbelief. For a moment, he wasn't seeing the cabin anymore. He was seeing a car exploding in a mall parking lot, the girl he loved vanishing in a ball of flame.

"Iola," he heard himself whisper.

Rita's screaming brought him back to the present. She had vaulted out of her seat and was running blindly back along the road to the cabin.

He gave chase, running in front of her to get her to stop.

It was as though he were invisible. Rita rammed right into him, and tried to keep going.

Joe wrapped his arms around her as she tried to pull free. Now he could hear what she was yelling. "No, no, no! Dad! *Dad!*"

"Dad?" Joe's grip slackened as he stared at Rita in amazement.

But Rita stayed where she was, sobbing wildly. "He wasn't my uncle," she choked. "That was my father down there—and now he's dead!"

Chapter

9

FRANK HARDY HAD just circled his way through the woods so he would come out behind the cabin.

It was dead ahead, masked only by a few trees. He had just started for it, when he heard a twig snap nearby. To his strained nerves, the sound was as loud as a gunshot. Frank froze behind a tree. Twigs didn't break by themselves. They snapped when something—or *someone*—stepped on them.

Then came the explosion!

It blasted Frank like a rag doll, tossing him off his feet and back against the trunk of a tree.

Later he groggily opened his eyes. The last thing he remembered was the blast. He must have been knocked out. The question was, for how long? He rubbed the back of his skull. His whole body was sore, covered with pine needles and debris from the explosion. He lay still, checking his arms, legs, and ribs for broken bones.

At last, he hobbled to his feet. Everything was quiet, except for the wind moving through the treetops.

He steadied himself, then moved ahead. Reaching the clearing, he saw that the cabin had been totally destroyed. Little remained but some shattered timber and stone, some bent and charred tin cans—and no signs of life.

"Too late—just a few minutes too late," Frank said to himself, not having heard the Jeep pull away. "I came so close to catching up with Joe, and now he's gone. No one could have survived this."

His hands were clenched so tightly, his fingernails dug into the flesh of his palms.

Joe led a shocked Rita back to the Jeep, which sat on the top of a hill. Below, smoke still hovered over the area where the cabin had been.

She tried to pull free, and he had to restrain her.

"I can't leave him there!" she said, her voice shaken.

"He's gone," Joe said roughly. "Dead, just like Iola," he added under his breath.

But Rita heard. "Who's she?"

Joe lowered his eyes. "A girl I loved. She was killed in a car bombing." He helped Rita into the

Jeep. Then he got behind the wheel. "I couldn't help her. But I can help you, Rita," he said quietly. "I can get you out of here, to safety."

She covered her face with her hands and began to sob. Her body heaved with each surge of grief. Joe leaned over and took her in his arms.

"We can't stay here," he told her gently. "Whoever set that explosion probably saw us leave and will come looking for us."

Afraid to make any noise, Joe released the brake and clutch, so the Jeep would roll silently down the hill. As it gained some speed, Joe nudged the brake pedal so it wouldn't go too fast.

He glanced at Rita. Her head was thrown back, tears streaming down her cheeks.

Joe steered the Jeep around some curves as it descended the hill. Reaching a flat stretch of road, Joe pushed in the clutch, threw the Jeep into second, and allowed the engine to drop-start and ignite.

Rita gained control of herself, taking deep breaths and wiping her eyes.

"There are some things you should know," she said in a choked voice.

"A whole lot of things, I bet."

She sighed. "It's true. Well, you know that Uncle Delbert is—was my father."

"Why all the secrecy?" Joe asked.

"Because there was a contract out on his life, that's why," Rita explained.

"Who was your dad, really?" Joe asked.

"My father's name was Mark Tabor," Rita said. "He was a businessman who was approached by some organized crime types. They wanted him to go along with a construction scheme to defraud the government out of a lot of money."

"Nice," Joe said sarcastically.

"Dad had a building supply business. Concrete and steel. The mobsters wanted him to overprice the cost of supplies needed for some big public building. Then the mobsters were going to charge the government for the inflated costs and pocket the difference. It would've meant millions and millions in illegal profits."

"But your dad wouldn't go along with it," Joe suggested.

"Well, actually," Rita said, "he did go along with the scheme. But only after he had notified the authorities. They asked him to help gather evidence."

"You mean, he was sort of a double agent," Joe said.

Rita nodded. "Right. After the mobsters were arrested, they figured that they'd get off, since there was no hard evidence against them. But they didn't know about my dad. He testified at the trial, and the mobsters were convicted and sent to prison."

"Which put your dad's life in jeopardy," Joe said.

"Yes. During the trial, right before Dad was

set to testify, my mother disappeared. Kidnapped." Her voice shook. "Murdered. When Dad hired a detective and found out that my mother was already dead, he went ahead." Rita began to weep again. "And now both of my parents are dead. And I hate the people who did it!"

Joe brought the Jeep to a stop. He held Rita, trying to console her, until she calmed down.

"I'm sorry," she said.

"You have nothing to apologize for," Joe told her.

"After the trial the authorities knew that his life and mine were in danger," Rita explained. "So, as part of the witness protection program, they gave us new identities. But the mobsters maneuvered for a new trial on a technicality, and started tracking us down so we couldn't testify. We ran—until we finally settled here."

"But someone just found your dad," Joe said.

"It won't do them any good," Rita said. "I know as much about the scheme as he did."

"I think they know that, too. That bomb was meant to kill both you and your dad."

Rita nodded grimly. "Well, they missed me. And I'll have my chance to convict them."

"Right," Joe agreed, starting the Jeep again. "But they'll have checked and know that you got away. And that makes *you* the new target!"

Back at the cabin, Frank Hardy prowled

around the smoking remains. There was little that hadn't been destroyed. He found the twisted remains of a pistol and rifle and the charred bones of only one body! The skeleton was too small to be Joe's—Joe must have survived! There was no sign whatsoever that his brother had been in the blast.

Joe had to be alive! And the girl with him.

Frank turned again to the remains of the cabin for a closer look. Bending down, sorting through the rubble with a stick, he found the remains of a thrown satchel charge—an old-fashioned kind of bomb, but a professional one.

Frank looked out on the road. The Jeep was gone! That was how they got away, he decided. But why didn't I hear the Jeep? Then he remembered—he had been deep in the woods then, circling around to the cabin. Frank quickly retraced his path through the woods. If Joe had gotten away in the Jeep, Frank had to get back to his car—and fast. He burst out of the woods, and climbed his way up to the highway above. There he flagged down a passing car.

"Can you give me a lift to Cripple Mine?" he asked. "I was hiking, and got turned around."

"Hop in," said the driver, a middle-aged man with a grizzled beard. "Folks get lost around here all the time," he said. "They wander off in the trees and lose their bearings."

"Yeah," Frank said. "That's what happened to me."

"Well, you be careful next time," the driver warned Frank. "Most anything can happen here in the high country if you don't know what you're doing."

Frank nodded silently. Up ahead he saw the spot where he'd hidden his rental car. "This will be fine," he told the man.

The driver laughed. "Don't want to admit somebody brought you back, huh?" But he good-naturedly pulled off the road. Frank thanked him and got out. "Would you know where I can find a phone?" he asked, leaning back into the car.

"There's a general store, oh, six miles up the road. It'll be on your right, on the river side," the driver said. "You can't miss it."

"And the sheriff," Frank added. "Where is his headquarters?"

"Well," the driver said, "that would be in Corralville. As the crow flies, it's not too far. But it's quite a drive from here—the mountains get in the way."

"I understand. Thanks again," Frank said.

Frank waited for the motorist to drive away, then he climbed in the rental car. It was time, he realized, to report to his father what had happened.

He drove to the general store, which looked like an old fishing lodge. Pulling into the parking lot, Frank went inside.

A couple of old-timers were standing around, talking about the weather and trout fishing. They

73

were dressed in plaid flannel shirts and corduroy trousers. Each wore a battered fishing hat complete with hooks and lures. Frank got a sandwich and a soda, then found a pay phone in the back.

He called home collect. His father accepted the call and immediately began to yell at him.

"Your twenty-four hours ran out this afternoon," Fenton Hardy growled. "You should have been home already. Now we're stuck here worrying about you, as well as your brother."

"Dad, I'm sorry, but there was no time to call. I had a lead on Joe and took off after him. I did see him and nearly caught up with him," Frank told his father.

"Where is he? And where exactly are you?" Fenton Hardy demanded.

"I'm in a general store in the mountains," Frank said. "I wish I could give you good news about Joe. But I just don't know for sure. Something terrible did happen. I found a cabin where, I believe, Joe was staying. Just as I was about to reach it, it was blown sky-high."

"What?"

"It was awful," Frank said. "I searched thoroughly and I'm almost positive he wasn't in it. But I think your witness might be dead. Did he live in a cabin?"

"He lived in a cabin about a mile from a place called Cripple Mine. And there should have been another person there—he had a daughter."

"Would the hit man have wanted to kill the daughter, too?" Frank asked.

"I would assume so, but let's not rush to conclusions," his father said worriedly. "A stove or gas leak might have caused that explosion."

"Dad, that explosion was no accident!"

"We can't know for sure," Fenton said. "I've just gotten word from a pretty good source that the hit man I sent Joe to warn the witness about is off the case. My source says it was just a wild-goose chase."

Frank shook his head. "Dad, I really think the man may have gotten to the witness. The explosion in that cabin was made by a satchel charge— very professional."

The silence that followed was so long, Frank thought he'd lost his connection. But Fenton Hardy finally spoke again. "In that case, we have no choice about keeping this secret. His daughter is in grave danger. I'm calling in the local police and the FBI right now!"

"Great," said Frank. "I'll get off the line." But even as he hung up, his brief flash of optimism faded.

There would be a lot of lawmen out looking for the hit man. But could they find him before he found the girl—and Joe?

Chapter

10

IT WAS LATE afternoon when Frank headed off toward Corralville, speeding along a steep and curving mountain road.

The sheriff was the nearest local law, and Joe would probably go there to report the blast at the cabin. It might be a slim hope, but it was the best one that Frank had.

As Frank drove, he weighed his evidence again. He was certain he had seen Joe going into the cabin. After the blast, he had found no traces of Joe in the rubble and debris. And the Jeep had disappeared.

Therefore, Joe couldn't be dead. He just couldn't be! Frank tried to shake that possibility from his mind, but it lingered like a bitter aftertaste.

Frank pushed on a little faster into the now deepening twilight. The mountain road was un-lit—a series of unending, twisting curves. Still, Frank kept his foot on the gas. When he finally hit a short stretch of straight road, he pushed the accelerator to the floor.

That was when his headlights caught something dead ahead in the road. Frank stared. A Jeep! It looked like the Jeep from the cabin!

He slammed on his brakes too late—surprise had slowed his reflexes. His car rammed into the rear of the Jeep, and Frank went bouncing against the steering wheel. Only his seat belt kept him from sailing through the windshield.

Frank tore loose from his belt and tried to open his door as the Jeep slowly rolled off the road, tumbling into a dry canyon floor below!

''No!'' Frank shouted, struggling with his door to get out. He shouldered the door again and again, throwing himself at it until it finally gave way.

Frank slid out of the car and dashed to the trunk. Unlocking the lid, he rummaged for a flashlight. Badly shaken and aching from the crash, he limped to where the Jeep had rolled off.

''Hey! Anybody down there?'' he shouted.

There was no response.

Frank flashed the flashlight beam down at the Jeep, which was turned over on its side. He played the light around, looking for any movement. But he saw nothing except the wreck itself.

Finding a sketchy path, he started down the steep hillside. The slope was slippery with gravel and bits of rock, and Frank nearly lost his footing more than once. For one horrible moment, his feet started sliding, and he had to grab a boulder to break his fall. The flashlight nearly went flying.

Finally hitting bottom, he found himself in a sandy ravine, perhaps a dried riverbed. Flashing the light back up at the road he inspected the steep, treacherous hill he had come down.

Then he limped toward the Jeep. "Joe?" He looked hard where the flashlight cast its beam, but saw nothing move.

He was almost afraid of what he'd find at the half-overturned jeep. But when he reached it, he found the Jeep empty. "This is weird," he said to himself. "If he's not here, where is he?" Frank swept the area with the flashlight again, but saw nothing but sand and brush.

The hood of the Jeep was loose, and Frank peeked in. "What's going on?" he muttered, staring at the place where the ignition wires had been torn out. That had to have been done by hand—the rest of the engine hadn't been damaged by the fall.

Leaning over the engine, Frank heard some

noise from the road above. He turned the flashlight upward—but again saw nothing.

He turned back to the Jeep. Nothing.

On the road above Frank, two figures moved out from behind the large boulder where they'd been hiding.

"I still don't understand how we ran out of gas," Rita said to Joe.

"Ask him." Joe pointed to the dark-haired scavenger below in the ravine.

"We could've driven over a rock or something that punctured the tank," Rita suggested.

"Up to a couple of minutes ago, I would have agreed," Joe whispered. "Now I think we're dealing with a professional killer—a guy who wanted us dead back at the cabin. But he couldn't stop us because his car was up on the road. So he punctured our gas tank, so we would be stranded in the middle of nowhere. Then he just drives up and finishes us off. You saw the way he hit the Jeep at a perfect angle, so it would roll into the canyon. And now he's down there, searching for our bodies!"

Rita crouched very still, watching the man climbing over the Jeep. "You mean that's the guy who murdered my father?" she asked.

Joe nodded. "He's a real pro. Look how easily he found us! He knew we'd run out of gas. What he didn't count on was our leaving the Jeep." Joe waved the ignition wires at Rita. "I took these out just so no one could steal the car. But he moved it right off the road."

"What should we do?" Rita asked. "He probably has a gun."

"You can bet on that," Joe said grimly. "I've been trying to figure some way to capture him. But I'm not going to get myself shot trying it."

Rita motioned toward the "killer's" car, resting against the rocky wall. "We could hide in the back and ambush him when he returns."

"We could," Joe agreed. "But we'd have to move pretty fast to nail him before he got a shot off."

"What are we going to do?" she asked.

"I don't know—and we don't have much time to come up with anything. I figure he'll look around for a few minutes more. Then he'll decide that we got away somehow and come after us again." Joe looked at her desperately. "It's a case of him or us, Rita!"

"But if we can't capture him, how can we"— she faltered on the word—"kill him?"

"Look," Joe said, pointing just up the road.

"What am I supposed to see?" Rita asked.

"That big boulder right on the lip of the canyon," Joe told her. "I bet I can start it down the hill."

"You mean a rock slide?" Rita asked.

Joe nodded. "Granted, a rock slide may not be fair, but it is effective."

Rita stared up at the night sky, struggling with

the idea. "My father always tried to play by the rules, and look where it got him. Chased down and hounded into the wilderness. His wife and finally himself killed," she said quietly.

"You said this wouldn't be very fair. Well, neither was throwing a bomb in our cabin." She looked Joe in the eye. "Let's do it!"

Rita and Joe rested against the big boulder and dug in with their feet. Then with all their strength they leaned back into it. It started to wobble.

Below, Frank stopped his search when he heard a low grinding noise. He looked up at the noise. It grew louder and louder, until a deafening rumble filled the air.

Frank lifted his flashlight—and shrank back. The gigantic boulder rolling down the side of the ravine was picking up speed and loosening other rocks. He was in a direct path with it.

He jumped back. A shower of gravel and pebbles pelted him on the head and chest. One rock struck his arm with stunning force and his hand went numb, forcing him to drop the flashlight. It hit against the ground with a thud, and the beam died.

Frank turned around and ran. How could he escape this trap?

Joe and Rita followed the boulder as it tumbled toward the Jeep.

Rita hid her head against Joe's chest as the deafening noise increased.

Joe rubbed her back, trying to calm her. He could feel her heaving with fear. "That should take care of him!" he said.

His words were nearly drowned out by the sound of boulders crashing against the canyon floor.

Chapter

11

FRANTICALLY TRYING TO outrace the thundering rock slide, Frank dashed for the far wall of the canyon. He scrambled up the steep rocky face on his hands and knees, trying to secure toeholds and handholds. His numb arm slowed him as he dragged himself up.

Now I know how a target in a shooting gallery feels, he thought as rock fragments *pinged* off the canyon wall. He tried to pull himself up with his bad arm, but it betrayed him. Frank slipped down. He yanked with his good arm and just cleared the spot where a stone smashed against the wall.

Frank struggled upward as the rock slide buried the Jeep. Vibrations brought more rocks down—on both sides of the canyon. As he clawed his way to safety, Frank had to hug the wall, covering his head and neck. Minislides rattled over him. Stones tore at his handholds, bashing his body with the force of punches. Rock dust choked him.

Then, as suddenly as the slide had begun—it stopped. A cloud of dust settled on Frank as he clung precariously to a ledge, waiting for aftershocks. But, after a moment, the night was eerily still.

Frank dragged himself to his feet, fighting to catch his breath. "*That* was no accident," he muttered to himself.

As if to confirm Frank's suspicions, a mechanical noise came from the road above him. A car engine. Frank's rental car? He lay low, just in case a light might pan the ravine below. Instead he heard someone gas the car, rev the motor, and drive away.

Frank groaned. He was much too far away to make any effective objection to the theft.

He sat up and started scouting his surroundings. The Jeep at the bottom of the ravine had disappeared, buried under tons of boulders and rocks.

But Frank now had a suspicion as to why he had found the Jeep empty. Imagine the nerve of that killer, he thought. He's done something to Joe and the girl and driven off in their Jeep!

Then when the Jeep stalled, he set up a trap, sure to lure any motorist to certain death in the ravine.

Frank's face went grim as he realized what he had just thought. Joe could be dead!

But Frank had survived and that gave him a temporary edge over the man.

"Some edge." Frank snorted. "No flashlight. No map. No car. But I'll have the advantage of surprise if I can run fast enough to catch up with him," he said ironically.

The killer hadn't even bothered coming down for a closer look. He'd just assumed that the rockslide had done Frank in.

Frank wished he hadn't dropped the flashlight because the darkness made for a slow climb. Only the dimmest starlight penetrated the deep ravine.

Carefully, Frank stepped across the still-shifting boulders, which now filled the canyon floor. "This could have been my grave," he muttered. Another climb up the opposite wall brought him to the deserted road above.

He started walking down the road. In his mind he recreated the map he had left in the car. As far as he could remember, the road got narrower and more winding, until it curved around a flat stretch of private land.

Concluding that he could save time by cutting across the land, Frank ducked under barbed wire and set off across a patch of grassy flatland. It was relatively easy for him to find his way.

About halfway across, he heard something large stirring nearby. The rising moon threw light on the scene. He laughed to find himself in the midst of a herd of cows. Apparently he was crossing private grazing land.

Quietly he moved past the herd, trying not to disturb the beasts. Up ahead he saw some lights. A ranch house? No, the lights were moving. A car. His calculations had been right! By going cross-country he had saved himself miles of walking.

Frank broke into a trot, then a run, trying to reach the road before the car passed. He ducked under another barbed wire fence and hid himself in some tall grass by the roadside.

The car approached, its headlights on bright. Frank squinted, so the glare wouldn't destroy his night vision. The car was almost on top of him before he recognized it. It was his own rental car!

Frank strained to see the driver, wanting to be able to identify the hit man. The face behind the wheel was revealed by the moonlight—his brother!

"Hey!" Frank shouted, getting to his feet and running into the road. "Stop! Joe! Stop! Stop!"

The car's brakes screeched as the wheels locked. It slowed to a stop.

"Joe! It's me, Frank!" he called, running toward the car.

The car did a three-point turn and slowly returned to Frank like a lumbering beast. Frank was engulfed by the headlights. The car stopped, but the engine was left to idle.

Joe warily got out and planted his feet. Instinctively, his hands rose to a defensive position. The face approaching him looked familiar.

Joe tensed, trying to place the face of the stranger walking toward him. He knew he had seen it often—but where? Those confusing dreams flashed again. The dark-haired guy who struggled against him. That grim face, aiming a gun!

"I was afraid you'd gotten away from me—that I'd never catch up with you," Frank said, smiling.

That was all Joe needed to hear. He rushed like a charging bull, tackling his enemy before he could pull his gun. Both of them went spilling into a dry gully off the road.

Joe rode his enemy down, keeping him on the bottom as they slid, choking in the dust. Maybe he'd be able to overpower this hit man, bring him in to justice. . . .

But when they jolted to the bottom, Frank Hardy managed to twist free. "What are you doing?" he yelled. "Don't you—"

His words were cut off when Joe threw a handful of dust into his face. Frank clawed at his eyes, and Joe tackled him again.

Joe knocked his blinded adversary flat. As long as he couldn't draw a weapon, they could fight on fairly even terms.

But even blinded, this guy was dangerous. Before Joe could pin his arms, his enemy lashed out with a karate blow and knocked Joe flat.

Joe shook his head once quickly, as another flash of memory came to him. He remembered another blow like that, one that knocked him out as he had tried to run to the burning car where Iola was trapped.

Joe threw himself at his adversary. He didn't care anymore about hidden weapons. He just wanted to smash that face!

Frank scrambled backward, trying to block his brother's wild onslaught. Fists, elbows, and knees pounded at him in a whirlwind attack. Frank ducked as a knockout blow grazed his ear instead of connecting with the side of his head. "Have you gone crazy?" he gasped.

But Joe just kept swinging with lunatic strength.

"Okay, you asked for it." Frank swept his leg around, catching Joe behind the knees. Joe dropped to the ground, just barely bracing himself on his hands. Frank fell on him and his hands darted to the pressure points on the neck. First he'd get Joe calmed down. Then he'd ask him what was going on.

But Joe wasn't finished yet. When he felt the fingers clamping down on him, he twisted with all his might, unleashing a right-handed haymaker from the ground up.

Frank saw the blow coming and tried to block it. But he used the arm that had been injured in the rockslide—the arm that had gone numb. It was still weak, and Joe's punch brushed by it to land right on the point of Frank's chin.

Joe grinned in triumph as he watched his enemy's head snap back, his legs go limp, his entire body slump bonelessly to the ground. "Get up!" Joe shouted, grabbing his enemy's shirt. "You killed Iola. You killed Rita's father! Get up and fight!"

He tried to lift his adversary to his feet but the dark-haired guy was dead weight. Joe let him fall hard against the ground.

He'd beaten him! All he had to do was tie him up, and bring him to the sheriff. . . .

But yet another memory was triggered—Joe charging out of some woods, pistol in hand, stopping when he saw the dark-haired guy sprawled motionless on the rocks, a big red stain on his shirt. Joe remembered how he had felt then—how upset he had been.

Upset? Over an enemy being shot? How could that be? This guy was a filthy murderer, a killer for hire! In a flash Joe decided there was only one way to stop him from ever killing again.

Joe picked up a large, flat rock, raising it over his head.

"This is it!" he snarled. "This time I'll finish you!"

Chapter

12

"WHAT'S GOING ON?" a voice called down from the road. "Wait! What are you doing? Stop!"

It was Rita. Joe heard her slide frantically down the gully, rush to him, and grab his arm. Joe let her pull the rock away, somehow glad for the interruption. His arms dropped to his sides.

Rita stooped and looked at the dark-haired guy passed out cold. She checked his pulse, shaking her head when she saw the blood on his face.

"What are you doing?" Joe asked.

"What does it look like?" Rita snapped. "He's got a split lip and a bloody nose. And I'm trying to help him!"

"I wouldn't get too close to him, Rita. He could be faking. We know he's a killer!"

"*Maybe* he's a killer. We don't know for sure,"

she said. "And he's still a human being. We can't just let him bleed."

"I go with 'An eye for an eye.' " Joe wiped the sweat and dust from his forehead with the back of his hand.

"Look at him lying there," Rita protested. "He's young. He could be your brother. Why, he even looks like you."

Joe stumbled back a few steps, confused. His mind was a jumble. What was going on here? Why was he relieved that Rita had stopped him from killing the dark-haired guy? Was he losing his mind?

Rita took a clean tissue from her pocket. She gently dabbed at the guy's mouth and nose, cleaning him as well as she could, making his breathing easier. "We can't leave him here," she said quietly. "He's badly hurt."

Joe stared at her. "You're not thinking of taking him with us, are you?"

"Why not?"

"I'll tell you straight out, Rita, I wouldn't want him behind me in the car while I was driving. He wants to *kill* us."

"We could tie him up," Rita suggested.

"We don't have anything to tie him with." Joe turned and climbed up toward the road. After a moment he turned and saw that Rita had not moved.

"We're going to leave him," he said. "By the

94

time he comes around, we'll be safely out of here." With that, Joe continued on his way.

Climbing up from the gully, he reached Frank's rental car and climbed in. He sat, waiting for Rita.

After a minute Rita silently slid into the car. "Are you really going to leave him down there?" she asked.

Joe's answer was to turn over the engine, put the car into gear, and drive off.

When Frank came around it took him a moment to realize where he was. He lay on his back, his body aching. Above him, the sky was radiant with the full moon shining. He tried to sit up but slipped back, feeling ill. The memory of his recent fight rose before him, and he felt sicker.

What happened to Joe? Frank wondered. He tried to kill me! Has he been brainwashed? He didn't even know who I was. I was fighting a robot!

Gingerly, Frank forced himself to sit up, waiting for the cobwebs to clear from his head. "What a mess!" he muttered. "The good news is that Joe is alive. But the bad news is that Joe must think that I'm the hit man!"

Swaying to his feet, Frank took a few wobbly steps, testing his ankles and knees. They still worked. He climbed up to the road again and set off.

To take his mind off his pains, Frank concentrated on inventing a new plan for finding and saving Joe. But he had no edge, nothing to work with. Alone in the Rocky Mountains at night, he had only his wits to help him. This was a time when he really could use Joe's help—but Joe, apparently, was on the other side.

The road began to slope up, and Frank walked for what seemed like hours. He was making some progress, but could never catch Joe on foot. No cars passed for Frank to flag down. No, he was on his own—on foot—whether he liked it or not.

The road forked, and Frank stopped to decide which way to go. He couldn't remember his map this far along. The left-hand route remained paved and appeared to snake up into the mountains, the right-hand route was dirt-covered, heading down into a large valley.

From his vantage point, Frank saw a small pool of light on the valley floor—not large enough to indicate a town, but light nonetheless.

It could be a place where he could find help. Besides, he had to take the easier route. So Frank took the road down into the valley.

As Frank approached the lights, they became brighter and more distinct. They were from some kind of building off the road in the near distance.

Frank quickened his pace, breaking into a hobbling run.

Just before he finally arrived, he stopped and leaned against an old fence to catch his breath.

He was at an old truck stop, left over from the days when this road had been the only one.

"I can't go in there looking like this," Frank said to himself. So he took a moment to comb through his hair with his fingers, then dusted and smoothed out his clothing. He wiped the blood off his face. Even with this effort, he still felt like the Wild Man of the Mountains.

Walking past a couple of antique gas pumps, he headed into a beat-up diner with flickering neon lights. There were no trailer trucks in the gravel parking lot, just an old pickup and a Highway Patrol car.

Frank entered the diner and smiled in surprise. The place was spotlessly clean. The linoleum floor shone with wax. The counter and stools were polished. Tubes of neon lights raced across the ceiling. Along the window wall were several booths. An old jukebox stood in one corner. Near it was a pool table and a rack of cue sticks.

The counterman, tall and skinny, with thin hair slicked back, wiped his hands on an apron, eyeing Frank. "Howdy, stranger," he said with a western twang.

He reached behind the counter for a coffee pot, and freshened the cup for a heavyset highway cop sitting on a far stool. As he leaned forward, he muttered something to the cop, who turned around and looked at Frank.

Obviously, the patrolman was not impressed by Frank's bedraggled condition. The lips went thin on his heavy face, and he crossed his arms across his chest. A metal bar pinned below his badge indicated that the cop's name was Higgins.

Patrolman Higgins didn't say a word. He merely glared at Frank as if he suspected Frank were an escaped convict or something.

Frank was so distracted that he nearly jumped when the counterman appeared before him.

"Sit anywhere you want," the man said, handing Frank a menu.

Frank took a seat in a vinyl-covered booth.

"You just take your time," the counterman said with a grin. "As you can see, the kitchen isn't exactly swamped with orders." With that, he returned to Higgins.

"You wouldn't believe my night so far," Higgins said. "Just before I pulled in here, I got an all-points bulletin over the radio. Dispatch said keep an eye out for a young guy with blond hair traveling with a girl. And get this—they said there was a hit man, some professional trigger-puller, loose in the area."

Higgins twisted his stool and gave Frank another hard look. "Didn't hear you come driving in, son," he said.

"No. My car broke down up the road," Frank said. "I think the clutch went out—the old wreck just died on a hill. So I left it and walked here."

"Is that right?" Higgins said.

"Is there a bus coming by?" Frank asked. "I need to get to the county seat."

"Bus service was stopped on this route months ago," the counterman broke in. "No profit left. Too bad about your car."

"What about that pickup out front?" Frank asked. "Could I rent it for a day or two?"

"Sorry," the counterman said. "That's mine, and I need it to get home.

"I really have to get somewhere—fast. It's a matter of life and death." Frank looked hopefully at the highway patrolman. "Do you think—"

"Sorry, son." Higgins didn't sound very sorry at all. "My patrol takes me in the opposite direction. You'll just have to sit tight till morning when a wrecker can help you."

From the look on Higgins's face, Frank wondered if he might be seeing a posse of local lawmen, first. He didn't dare tell the cop about Joe for fear Joe had really flipped out. Joe could attack this guy, as he had Frank, and be killed. No, Frank decided. I'll just cool it and find Joe on my own.

Then he looked up again. "I guess you're right," Frank told Higgins and the counterman. "My old wreck isn't going anywhere." He grinned. "So I might as well eat. How about a steak, baked potato, the works?"

The counterman went into the kitchen, and Higgins returned to his coffee. Frank stared out the window anxiously.

A big plate of food soon appeared on the table. Frank tore into the steak. He hadn't realized how hungry he was. "Delicious," he told the counterman. "Mind if I take this outside? I'd like to eat under the stars."

"Suit yourself," the counterman said with a chuckle.

Frank picked up the plate and went outside. Glancing back inside, he noticed that the counterman and Higgins were paying no attention to him. There was no place for him to go, anyway.

Frank strolled past Higgins's car, number twenty-eight, and dropped to one knee, glancing nervously to see if either man was looking out. They weren't. He shoved the baked potato into the cruiser's exhaust pipe. Then, putting the plate on the ground, he walked over to the pickup and climbed inside.

Ducking low, he yanked at the ignition wires. It was a nerve-racking job, hot-wiring a truck in full view of the owner. If either of the two inside glanced his way—

The motor caught, backfired, and finally turned over. Frank leapt behind the wheel. He pushed in the clutch and punched the stick on the floor into reverse.

The noise caught the attention of the two men inside the diner.

Just as Frank was backing away, Patrolman Higgins burst from the door, hauling his service revolver from its holster.

"Hold it!" Higgins yelled, dropping into the classic marksman's firing-line position.

The gun in his hand looked about the size of a cannon, and it was aimed straight at Frank's head.

"Stop!" Higgins yelled again. "Or I shoot!"

Chapter

13

"COME ON, YOU old piece of junk!" Frank shouted, stomping on the pickup's gas pedal. He spun the wheel and the truck squealed out of the parking lot. A storm of gravel flew from under the tires. Frank hoped the gravel might block Patrolman Higgins's aim.

He glanced back for a second, expecting to see a bullet with his name on it. Instead, he saw the counterman shove Higgins's arm up. Frank gave a sigh of relief. Apparently, the counterman didn't want any bullet holes in his precious pickup.

Frank pushed the steering wheel, as if that would somehow make the pickup gain some speed. "Come on, you old clunker! We can make it."

In the rearview mirror, Frank saw Officer Higgins making for the highway patrol car. The counterman stood by the diner, waving his hands, jumping up and down.

"With my luck," Frank muttered, "I'll be arrested for stealing this hunk of junk *and* not paying for that steak."

The pickup groaned its way up a hill as the lights on Patrol Car 28 went on. In the mirror, Frank saw it roar out of the parking lot, spinning clouds of dust.

If I had to steal something, Frank thought, I should've stolen the patrol car, instead. At least it has some power.

He grinned at the image of Officer Higgins trying to chase him in the wheezing pickup. But his grin disappeared at the first scream of the siren behind him. Of course, he realized, stealing a patrol car would have landed me in jail.

Then he caught a glimpse of the revolving red lights on top of the cop-car closing the distance between them. Of course, if Higgins catches up with me, I'll *still* be in a ton of trouble!

Frank checked the rearview mirror again. The patrol car was gaining on him. Not too difficult, since the pickup speedometer was indicating a mere forty-five miles per hour. Higgins flashed his lights at Frank, insistently pointing to the side of the road.

The patrol car came so close that Frank could hear its roaring engine. Then Higgins's voice came blaring over the rooftop speaker:

"Okay, son, just pull over. Your little prank is finished. Pull over and there won't be any problem. Come on, kid, give yourself up and the judge might be more lenient."

"Oh, thanks a lot!" Frank said. His eyes desperately scanned the landscape ahead. If he could just make it to the top of the rise, he might be all right.

"Pull over right now!" Higgins barked. "I'm warning you, son. Right now! I'm counting to five, then I'll shoot your tires out! One, two, three—"

Frank pressed the accelerator pedal again, and the truck spurted over the rise. The patrol car did the same. By now, it was so close, it nudged the pickup on the rear bumper.

"I'm not going to pull this off," Frank said to himself, despairing. "Well, I gave it my best shot—"

Suddenly car 28 sputtered. Hearing the sound, Frank watched the scene in the rearview mirror. The patrol car jumped ahead, stopped, sputtered, jumped ahead again, and then died. Stone cold dead in the middle of the road!

Inside the patrol car, Higgins kicked the transmission back into park and turned over the ignition. The engine wouldn't catch. Over and over Higgins tried to start it—with no success. He slammed his hands against the dashboard in frustration, then picked up the mike.

"I'll get you, kid!" he roared after Frank.

Up ahead, putting some distance between Higgins and the pickup, Frank grinned with relief. The potato *had* blocked the patrol car's exhaust pipe. And the exhaust gases, with nowhere else to go, had damped down the engine.

"All *right!*" Frank whispered, congratulating himself.

But his grin soon faded. He'd lost a lot of time. And he wasn't going to make any of it up, chugging along in this heap. Joe would be long past the county seat before Frank even got there—unless the hit man caught him first.

That thought set Frank to work like a madman, squeezing every bit of speed from the pickup. The road began to rise and fall like a roller coaster. At the top of an especially high hill, Frank pushed in the clutch and slipped the gears into neutral. Using the weight of the truck and the steep decline, he soon had the pickup rolling along faster than sixty miles an hour.

Cruising well ahead on the road, Joe glanced over at Rita. She was curled asleep, her body turned toward the seat. Joe's jacket covered her.

Joe tried to hold his eyes open. A few times he had found himself nodding out over the wheel. But he had forced himself to sit back and stare ahead. Joe wasn't sure how much longer that would work. He was exhausted.

Nudging Rita with his elbow, he asked, "Any idea how much farther to Corralville?"

She yawned and stretched. "How long have I been sleeping?"

"An hour and a half," Joe told her.

"We should be pretty close," she said. "Want me to drive?"

"Maybe so," Joe said. "I can't stay awake. But you know, maybe it's a good idea to enter Corralville in the morning, when the sheriff will be at his office."

"So what do you want to do?" Rita asked.

"Let's pull over and knock off a few Zs," Joe suggested. "We can hide the car off the road."

"All right," Rita said.

Joe slowed the car, then pulled off the highway onto a narrow dirt road. He followed the road as it passed some rangeland protected by barbed wire fences.

Figuring that they were safely out of sight, Joe pulled off the road into a patch of buffalo grass.

"Well, good night then," Joe said, turning off the engine.

Rita mumbled, already half-asleep.

Joe leaned against the driver's door and closed his eyes. His body was exhausted—but his mind wouldn't give up. The pictures in it weren't making a whole lot of sense, but they kept flashing.

If these are my memories, Joe thought, I must lead a pretty violent life. Faces kept appearing— a big, beefy blond guy, smiling. A heavyset guy who grinned a lot. An older man and woman—

his parents? And, of course, the dark-haired guy, laughing at him.

Joe forced himself to relax, closing his eyes. His breathing became more regular, his head tilted to one side. . . .

And then the dark-haired guy was leaping across the hood of the car. He pinned Joe with a cold stare as he coolly drew his pistol. He was every inch the pro. The gun was aimed right at Joe's head, the bullet tearing through the windshield.

Joe grabbed at the handle and rammed into the door. He had actually fallen out onto the grassy margin at the roadside before his eyes opened! Still shaken, he stared around the empty field, almost positive the hit man was still there.

"A dream," he whispered to himself. He glanced up into the car at Rita, who was still fast asleep.

"Boy," he muttered, "this girl could sleep through a hurricane."

He stood up and checked the dashboard clock. Apparently he had dropped off for an hour's rest, though it didn't feel like it.

Time to find the sheriff, Joe thought, and finally put an end to this nightmare.

Without waking Rita, he turned the key, started the engine, and began to follow the road back toward the highway.

Frank couldn't believe his luck. No one had

found him yet. Higgins had to have called the highway patrol. They were probably searching the major highways. No one would believe he'd stay in the area on a small road.

Frank was pretty tired though. He'd spent the past hour playing any game to stay awake. He did complicated math problems. He named, in order, every element in the periodic table. He sang the lyrics to every song he could remember. He tried to recall the name of every kid in his classes from elementary school. He began to recite the fifty states: Alabama, Alaska, Arizona, Arkansas, California, Colorado—Colorado!''

Frank couldn't believe his eyes. Pulling into the highway just ahead of him was a familiar car. His rental model—with Joe in the driver's seat!

No one would believe him, Frank thought to himself.

He slowed the pickup—not a difficult task—and allowed the rental car to gather some speed. The big problem was figuring out a way to approach Joe without turning him into a madman again.

I'll never catch up to him if he tries to pull away, Frank thought. My one advantage is that he won't recognize this truck. Maybe I can lure him back.

With that, Frank honked the horn a few times, drawing Joe's attention. When the rental car's brake lights went on, Frank whipped the pickup's steering wheel to the right. His idea was to fake a blowout and hope Joe would respond.

Frank held on, as the pickup skidded off the road. Quickly he looked up. Joe had gone for the bait! The rental car was turning around and approaching the pickup.

Frank opened the door and climbed out. Ready to take on Joe, if necessary.

The rental car stopped, catching Frank in its headlights.

Frank took a few steps toward the car. Good, it looked as if Joe would be reasonable.

Joe's suspicion turned to horror as he stared at the dark-haired guy appearing out of the predawn mist. "Oh, no!" he shouted, waking Rita.

He spun the steering wheel and floored the accelerator.

Frank leapt aside as the car swerved right through the area where he'd been standing. "Not *this* again!" he groaned, pulling himself up and rushing back to the pickup.

His tires screamed as he threw the truck into motion. The chase was on!

Chapter

14

BY THE TIME Frank had his pickup back on the road, the rental car had zoomed ahead. Frank chugged slowly behind.

"I'll never catch him," Frank told himself miserably. Still, what choice did he have?

Frank watched the taillights of the rental car disappear over a hill. All the tiredness that his momentary excitement had burnt away fell back onto him. What had gotten into Joe? he wondered.

If he were trying to warn Frank off, that rock-slide was far too deadly. Maybe Joe was somehow being forced to act hostile. But the beating he'd given Frank hadn't been acting. And he could have whispered an explanation during one of the clinches.

The pickup plowed along following the cloud of

dust raised by Joe's car. Frank was determined to make some sense out of his brother's weird behavior.

What would make Joe act this way? Frank asked himself.

Brainwashing? But Joe had only disappeared a couple of days. Frank couldn't believe he could have been brainwashed in such a short time.

Hypnotism? That might explain why Joe was so unexpectedly hostile. And it would explain why Joe might attack him but not finish him off. People under hypnosis couldn't be ordered to do things that they believed to be wrong. Frank shook his head. A hit man using hypnosis? That was just too bizarre.

Frank laughed at the image of a thug with a gun in one hand, saying, "You are in my power." He would wear a black mask, and a magician's turban—*turban!*

Frank's hands clenched the wheel as he remembered creeping up on the cabin in the woods. He'd seen a distant figure walking from the Jeep—a figure that had turned out to be Joe. But the first time he'd seen him, Frank thought the guy was wearing a turban. What if it wasn't a turban—but some kind of bandage on his head?

"Amnesia." Frank exhaled loudly. It made sense. Joe had looked pretty battered. He must have been bumped around a lot when his car was wrecked. What if Joe had bumped his head? Then Frank remembered the bloody tire iron, with the hairs caught on it. What if Joe had been *hit* on the head? What if he lost his memory?

What if he thinks I'm the hit man who's after him?

Frank gripped the wheel. He *had* to catch up with Joe.

"Slow down!" Rita shouted, pulling at Joe's arms. "We've lost him! He can't hurt us now!"

Joe glanced in his rearview mirror. She was right. The dark-haired killer and his pickup had fallen far behind. But Joe still kept the gas pedal down low. It might be irrational, but he swore to himself that he'd take no chances with that guy.

"Slow down! Please!" Rita pleaded as the car screeched around a sharp curve. "Do you want us to go off the road?"

Joe didn't answer her. And he didn't slow down.

"What's the matter with you?" Rita's voice rose. "Have you gone out of your mind?"

Joe twisted around to glare at her, wild-eyed.

"Look out!" Rita screamed.

He turned forward again. He was approaching a hairpin turn that was upon him right then. Slamming on the brakes, Joe twisted the wheel into the turn. The car screeched along a steel guardrail, which alone kept it from spilling down the steep rocky slope.

Joe fought to regain control of the car—and

himself. "I—I think we left some of our paint on that railing," he finally gasped.

They slowed down, then stopped.

Rita pried his hands off the steering wheel. "What happened back there?" she asked.

"Please, Rita," Joe begged, "don't tell me I've gone crazy. I saw him back there. The dark-haired guy. The hit man. He came walking right into our headlights. Smiling. *Smiling*. I couldn't take it. I had to get away."

He shook his head. "I guess I did go crazy, for a while. That was a foolish stunt I pulled. I could have gotten us killed."

"All the time, I keep getting flashes—pictures of that guy fighting with me, laughing at me. He stopped me from saving Iola. . . ." Joe's voice broke off.

Then he turned to Rita, whispering fiercely, "But he's not going to keep me from saving you!"

He shook his head. "I haven't been able to stop him yet. But I've just got to outplan him. Every time he's turned up, he's caught us by surprise. So this time we'll have to surprise him. *Really* surprise him.

"Let's take a look at the map."

Rita spread it out. "I know this stretch of road," she said, pointing at a line snaking through the mountains. "A few more miles and we'll clear these mountains. From there on it's a flat five-mile stretch into Corralville."

Joe examined the map very carefully. "What's this line here?" he asked suddenly, stabbing at the map with his finger.

Rita squinted, then nodded. "That's an old logging road, just at the edge of the mountains," she said. "I don't know if anyone even drives there. You can't really see it, it's hidden by some aspen trees."

"Perfect," said Joe. He started up the engine again and drove off.

Frank, making the best time he could, came wheezing downhill in his stolen pickup. Long before he had lost sight of the rental car.

"At the speed he took off, Joe will be in California before I make it to Corralville," he said, fuming.

"I hope somebody nails that hit man. Because *I* want first crack at my baby brother. I'll pound some sense into that thick skull of his." That got a laugh out of Frank. "Dr. Hardy's Amnesia Cure."

He eased the truck around a last curve, which provided a fine view of the valley below. Some six or seven miles off were the lights of Corralville.

Frank anxiously scanned the flat expanse of roadway. "Empty," he said. "Not a car out there. Joe must be in the town already—unless he went another way or just passed through."

Then he remembered the all-points bulletin that

had been posted for Joe. He also thought that there must be one out for him, too. "There's a sheriff in Corralville. Maybe *he* got hold of Joe."

Frank tromped the accelerator again, eager to reach Corralville.

The pickup whipped through the final turn, and the road began to flatten.

All of Frank's attention was on the road before him, so he barely noticed a churning sound erupting from a stand of aspens off to one side.

He turned when the sound got louder and saw a car come barreling into view—flashing straight at the pickup!

Frank tried to brake, tried to turn aside. But the onrushing car caught him broadside, smashing him off the road, into the ditch.

The last thing Frank remembered was his own brother, grim-faced at the wheel, ramming him!

Chapter

15

JOE HARDY BROUGHT his car out of the crash and fishtailed back onto the highway. He didn't even look back at the pickup he'd sent hurtling off the road. He was just happy that his car wasn't so badly damaged that it couldn't be driven. The door on Joe's side was sprung, and the whole front end was bashed in—but still the car drove.

Rita stared out the rear window as the truck landed on its side. "The gas tank didn't explode," she said. "I guess he'll be all right in there."

Joe nodded. "One thing's for sure. He's not going anywhere. The sheriff can pick him up."

Billboards advertising restaurants and motels clustered along the roadside, announcing that they were approaching Corralville. Then came signs announcing a decrease in the speed limit and a school crossing warning. A few minutes later they were stopped by a true sign of civilization—a traffic light.

Joe brought the car to a stop, steam billowing out of the engine, then he turned to Rita.

"So what's our plan?" she asked.

Joe peered through the spider's web of a windshield to see that night had given way to dawn. Daylight illuminated the road ahead. "The sheriff should be getting to headquarters soon," he said.

Rita nodded. "Right. Our best hope is to get the coded message to the authorities."

Joe patted his breast pocket, feeling the paper inside. "Yes."

Rita leaned back. "Thank goodness. Imagine, before long I'll be able to stop running. I'll be safe and free." She turned her head toward the window. "I'll look for the sheriff's office," she said.

But before Joe could get the car in gear, he had another memory flashes—a crooked sheriff aiming a gun at Joe's nose. "They pay me good money to take care of problems like you," the sheriff said. He remembered his muscles tensing for a hopeless spring—and the dark-haired guy warning him back. Then the two of them together had overpowered the corrupt lawman.

"The dark-haired guy *helped* me!" Joe muttered to himself.

"What?" Rita said. "Did you say something to me?"

Joe shook his head. "No, I was just thinking out loud."

"What about?" Rita asked with concern.

"Maybe going to the sheriff isn't such a good idea," Joe told her. "Maybe the right thing to do is turn back and see if that guy in the pickup is okay."

"Don't start acting crazy again!" Rita warned Joe. "We're so close—can't we just finish this thing and get on with our lives? Please? The sheriff isn't going to hurt us."

Joe forced the disturbing memory into the back of his brain.

"Okay," he said. "We'll go to the law."

Rita nodded in approval.

They topped a rise, and sprawling out before them in the sunrise was the town they'd been struggling to reach. Corralville, the county seat.

Rita looked around the dusty main street. "It's hard to believe Corralville was once one of the richest towns in the world," she said.

"This place?" Joe said in disbelief.

"They found silver in these hills," Rita said. "The whole town sprang up overnight. Hotels and gambling houses, fancy shops and saloons."

Joe looked at a sagging wooden building. "Didn't last, I guess."

Rita nodded. "The mines dried up, and most of the people left. Nobody comes here now—except people who get lost looking for the ski resorts."

"It is almost like a ghost town—especially at dawn," Joe said as they silently rolled along the empty streets.

They passed a few old wooden houses that lined both sides of the road. Then they reached the tiny downtown section. A school filled much of one block, and churches were set on various corners. They passed a gas station and a general store, a coffee shop and a garage. In the middle of the block Joe slowed the car to a crawl.

On one side was an old red brick county courthouse. And, across the street, next to the post office, was an unassuming one-story, yellow brick building with the words County Sheriff stenciled on the window.

Joe rolled to a stop and parked the car outside the sheriff's office. A light inside indicated that someone was on duty. He turned off the engine and glanced at Rita.

"Well," he said, "here we are."

Dawn found Frank stumbling over his own feet as he staggered along the road. He was moving as much to stay warm as to find Joe. The second task was surely hopeless—his brother was long gone.

Bruised and bone-weary, Frank challenged himself to keep his feet moving. He was shaken— not just by the physical batterings he had sustained, but by the realization that his brother could attack him so savagely in cold blood. Frank couldn't erase the memory of the look on his brother's face as his car rammed into him. He didn't even check to see what happened to me, Frank thought. It's got to be amnesia. But who does he think I am?

But that didn't matter right then. Joe was in trouble, and somehow, Frank had to catch up with him. He glanced at his watch. Twenty minutes since he'd pulled himself out of the wreck, and he'd gone only about a mile. At that rate, Frank could expect to hit Corralville in about an hour and a half. Maybe Joe would be there, with the sheriff. Or maybe by then, Joe would be ninety miles away.

Frank forced his legs to move faster, stumbling into an ungainly jog-trot. When he got to the sheriff's he could report what had happened and he could call his dad and maybe get some help for his brother.

He had reached the first set of billboards announcing Corralville when he heard the siren screaming behind him.

Frank dove off the road and lay low in some buffalo grass, out of sight. This is a great time for the Highway Patrol to catch up with me, Frank thought.

Well-hidden, he crawled to a spot which allowed him a clear view of the highway.

Barreling down the road was Highway Patrol Car 28, the one he had sabotaged at the truck stop.

Frank rose up at the exact moment the cruiser came rushing by. What he saw gave him a very bad feeling indeed.

That can't be, Frank thought. The man at the patrol car's wheel did not look like Officer Higgins. This cop had red hair and a sharp, needle-like nose. What was this guy doing in Higgins's car? And why was he breaking the speed limit to get to the county seat?

The image of the driving officer's red hair returned to Frank's mind. What if the guy in the car was an impostor?

Then whatever business he had in Corralville, he couldn't be up to any good.

Frank jumped back on the road, redoubling his pace. Trying to take his mind off the pain in his legs and the burning in his lungs, he tried to imagine how someone else could have ended up in Higgins's car. It was all too simple.

The redhead must have found Higgins right after his cruiser conked out. Catching the cop by surprise, he overpowered Higgins. Then, with the officer either stunned or dead, the guy must have figured out that something was blocking the car's exhaust system.

"Nice work," Frank told himself sarcastically. "I stopped Higgins all right. And in doing it, I may have given the hit man a perfect cover for his next killing."

Yes, the hit man! If his impostor theory were right, who else would be masquerading as a lawman? Frank almost stumbled again as that thought hit him. "If he gets to Joe and murders him, there will be only one person to blame. *Me!*"

Frank pushed back his horror. He lowered his head and forced more speed out of his oxygen-starved legs. Joe was *really* in danger now. He had to make Corralville, and right away. He *had* to!

Chapter

16

HALF AN HOUR later Frank Hardy was still stumbling along the road, wondering if he were running in place. Corralville seemed to be as far away as ever. Although his worry for Joe kept him plodding onward, he could feel his body betraying him. He was limping even more, and a catch in his side sent pain screaming through him with every step.

If Joe had stopped in Corralville, Frank was almost afraid of what he would find there. He might arrive to discover he had a score to settle with Joe's killer, Joe having died without even knowing who he was—

That nightmare vision spurred Frank into a slow-motion parody of a run. His body was just too wasted, too battered, too *tired* to perform the way Frank wanted it to.

Frank's feet hit a patch of loose gravel, and he lost his balance. He nearly fell flat on his face, but at the last instant he broke his fall, scraping his palms raw. "Great," he muttered, wincing at his new injury. "Can't I do *anything* right anymore?"

Pulling himself wearily to his feet, Frank spotted a vehicle on the road. It was coming toward him from Corralville. Frank tensed. Was it the highway patrol cruiser? Was the impostor making his getaway, heading back after finishing his job?

Frank thought he saw lights mounted on the top of the car. He glanced around desperately for some sort of weapon, even a rock to throw. He couldn't let this guy escape. But as the vehicle drew closer, he recognized the outlines of a tow truck.

Jumping up and down, waving his arms, Frank flagged it down. The tow truck rolled to a stop ahead of him, and Frank ran to it. He hopped onto the running board, leaning in the window. "Boy, am I glad to see you."

"What are you doing out here?" The driver's big, beefy face had a look that fell somewhere between scorn and suspicion. "You look like vulture meat, friend."

Frank ignored the sarcasm. "I really need a lift into Corralville," he said.

The man's eyes narrowed. "I tow cars. I'm not a taxi service."

But Frank knew that if this guy—Bert was

printed on his coverall—saw the wrecked pickup, his problems would only be starting. Bert would be sure to recognize a local truck—and he'd have to know that Frank had stolen it.

"Hey, give me a break," Frank said. "It's very important I get there as soon as possible. A matter of life and death."

"Look, kid," Bert said coldly. "If you're so eager to get to town, you can walk from here."

"You don't understand!" Desperate to convince the man, Frank reached through the window, grabbing Bert by the arm. Bert yanked himself loose and thrust open the door, knocking Frank off the running board and onto the ground.

Frank landed heavily. By the time he scrambled to his feet, Bert had jumped out of the truck. In his hand was a large, heavy wrench.

"I thought you looked suspicious," Bert growled, hefting the wrench. "Weird things going on. Sheriff tells me we got a hit man creeping around somewhere. And I bet he's you!"

Bert moved fast for a beefy guy. He charged Frank, swinging the wrench overhand, straight for Frank's head.

Frank threw his arms over his head, crossing them and locking the forearms together.

Bert's wrist smashed into Frank's block. He grunted in surprise and pain. Frank grabbed Bert's wrist and attempted to disarm him.

But the scrapes on his palms let him down, and Frank couldn't get a good grip. Bert tore loose.

"Smart boy, huh?" Bert stepped back and swung the wrench sidearm, aiming for Frank's shoulder.

He had expected Frank to back-pedal—but instead, Frank attacked! He rammed his forearms down, moving not for the wrench but for the arm that swung it.

Bert stared in surprise as his blow was again slowed. But this time, Frank clamped down on the arm with the wrench, capturing it between his left arm and his body. His right hand rammed up heel first into Bert's chin.

Bert's head snapped back, and his whole body followed, helped along by Frank's right foot behind his ankles. Bert hit the ground with a thud, and Frank leapt on him, his hands darting for pressure spots in his neck—

A moment later Frank was dragging the unconscious truck jockey to the side of the road. "So much for famous western hospitality," he said. "Sorry, Bert."

Dumping Bert in a safe spot, Frank dashed back to the tow truck and climbed in. The engine started on the first try, and soon Frank was whipping the truck in a tight U-turn. Pressing the accelerator to the floor, Frank quickly worked his way through the gears, speeding toward Corralville.

"I only hope that I'm not too late," he said to himself.

*　　*　　*

The county sheriff, a short bald man with a pot belly, kicked his cowboy boots up on the desk. He leaned forward and took a sip of coffee, eyeing Joe and Rita, who were seated across the desk.

"Now, let me see if I've got your stories straight," the sheriff said. He pointed at Rita. "You're telling me that you survived the explosion that wiped out the log cabin."

"That's right," Rita said. "The explosion that killed Mark Tabor, my father."

The sheriff ran a hand along his chin. "The papers on that cabin don't say anything about a Mark Tabor."

Joe interrupted impatiently. "She explained about all that. They're under the witness protection program."

That got him a dirty look from the sheriff. The lawman studied Joe slowly.

"You have to believe us!" Rita said. "We told you exactly what happened at the cabin. Doesn't that prove anything?"

"It shows you knew a lot more about the explosion than we told the press. More than any innocent person should know." The sheriff removed his feet from the desk, then he leaned forward, thrusting his face into Joe's. "Now you tell me you survived a car wreck near Cripple Mine, escaped the explosion, fought with the hit man, and brought this girl to me. Quite a story."

He leaned back in his chair again, trying to

look casual. "Now, what did you say your name was?"

"I'm telling you, I can't remember!" Joe said.

"How about some ID then?" The lawman's voice got harder.

"I must have lost it," Joe told him.

"Mighty convenient, not being able to tell me your name." The sheriff looked more suspicious now. "You have nothing you can show me?"

Joe then remembered the coded message in his pocket. "I've got something which may convince you," he said, reaching into his pocket. Mark Tabor had told him to bring it to the sheriff. Maybe the lawman could figure it out.

But Joe's pocket had not been the safest place to be during this adventure. To his horror, the paper came out as a crumpled mass, almost torn in two pieces. Joe tried to straighten it out, but the paper looked like a torn mess, its message illegible.

The lawman squinted at the paper, then looked at Joe. "This is all you've got to show?" he asked, trying hard not to smile.

"What about the hit man?" Joe said desperately. "He might still be out where we rammed his car. Can't you go and look around?"

"I will—soon as my deputy gets here." The sheriff glanced at his watch. "That'll be about an hour and a half. We'll check out your story."

"And what are we supposed to do in the meantime?" Joe asked.

"You may be important witnesses—or suspects—in a murder. I think you should stick around." He pointed to a door at the rear of his office, and fished out some keys with one hand.

Rita and Joe both leapt from their seats.

"You're going to lock us up?" Hands clenched, Joe took one step forward.

The lawman quickly unholstered his service revolver, pointing it at Joe. "I don't want any trouble," he said. "Now stand where you are, and keep your hands where I can see them."

Having no choice, Rita and Joe did as the sheriff instructed.

The lawman motioned them around the desk, keeping the pistol pointed at Joe. He unlocked the door he'd pointed at. "Okay, you two," he said. "Come this way."

Rita and Joe moved into the back and saw two separate holding cells. The lawman unlocked one cell and told Rita, "Make yourself comfortable, little lady. I've got a few phone calls to make."

Rita walked into the cell and the lawman closed and locked the door behind her. He then unlocked the neighboring cell and motioned Joe inside. "Remember," the lawman said, "no funny stuff."

Steaming with frustration, Joe entered the cell, standing with his back toward the lawman until the door closed and he heard the lock tumble shut.

The sheriff returned to his office, tossing the

keys on the desk before him. He tried to decipher the coded message again, but even an expert could make no sense of it now.

He reached out to pick up the telephone when he heard someone step up on the outside stoop. The front door opened, and a tall, thin, redheaded older man dressed in an ill-fitting highway patrol uniform entered. The man had a shotgun slung over his shoulder.

"Morning," the stranger said.

"I don't know you," the sheriff said, giving him a hard look.

"Nope. I'm the new man on the force," the stranger said. "Just dropped by to get acquainted."

"Then what's with the shotgun?" the sheriff asked, surprised at how old the stranger was.

"We're taking no chances, what with all the troubles around here lately," the redhead said, setting the weapon against a chair. "A scattergun might be just the thing to take care of some big-city hit man."

The sheriff grinned at that. "Yep," he said. "My little town isn't used to such a ruckus. And isn't it just like headquarters not to bother telling me about any extra patrols."

The stranger grinned back and chuckled. "Hey, sheriff, I noticed the rental car parked outside. You wouldn't happen to know where the occupants are?"

"Well, I have them under lock and key in the back," the sheriff boasted.

"You don't say," the stranger said with a nod. "Good work. I'll be sure to tell headquarters about you. I've been tracking those fugitives all night. How about a look?"

"Okay." The sheriff turned and unlocked the rear door. He swung it open. "See? They aren't going anywhere."

The stranger stood behind the sheriff, taking in the sight of Joe and Rita, locked in separate cells.

The sheriff was enjoying his moment of triumph. "See?" he said, gesturing at his prisoners. "All tight."

"Yup," the stranger echoed. "All tight." He swung the shotgun in a vicious arc, until the butt caught the sheriff in the back of the head.

Joe, Rita, and the stranger watched the sheriff topple to the floor.

Then the stranger brought the shotgun up to firing position.

"Now that the local law is asleep," the phony patrolman said, "I can finish up my real business!"

Chapter

17

FRANK ROARED ALONG the last mile to Corralville, maintaining the truck's speed as he raced down Main Street. The town was deserted so early in the morning, as if everything and everyone were in storage.

Like a movie set for a western, Frank thought. The final showdown.

Frank caught a glimpse of himself in the rearview mirror. He looked about as hard-faced and dangerous as any cowboy heading for a shootout.

His face only got harder as he sped along, searching for the sheriff's office. There it was, dead ahead and parked in front was patrol car 28. Right in front of that was the rental Joe had stolen from him. The bright morning sunlight reflected off the sheriff's office windows, denying Frank a look inside.

Frank continued past, pulling the tow truck around the corner and parking. He had to plan his next step very carefully. If the guy in the patrol car was an impostor, that meant the hit man was already in the sheriff's office. Wearing Higgins's uniform—even if it didn't fit—he could convince the sheriff that he was a legitimate lawman.

If Frank went storming in with accusations, the hit man would start shooting. Could he phone a warning in? No, the hit man might answer the phone.

Frank just didn't know what was going on inside the office. So he'd have to get the lawmen *out,* before he could go in. He needed some kind of diversion. But what?

All Frank had was whatever he could find in the tow truck he'd "borrowed" from Bert. He opened the glove compartment, but found nothing but papers and maps. Checking under the seat yielded a tool kit and a few spools of wire.

Frank climbed down from the cab and searched the back. He found only a set of jumper cables, some old oily rags, and a gasoline can. Shaking the can, he heard the gasoline slosh around inside. Instantly, his mind started planning.

"Hmmmm," he said. Not much to work with but— He had the glimmering of an idea. It was the best plan Frank could come up with in a hurry. And it *would* make a pretty spectacular diversion.

He removed the cap of the gasoline can and stuffed the oily rags inside, leaving only a tip of cloth to serve as a fuse. To this makeshift fuse he wrapped some wire, which he then attached to one end of the jumper cables. Before leaving the truck, Frank dug out a tire iron. Then, with his homemade bomb in one hand and the steel rod in the other, he approached the sheriff's office.

Frank crept up on the stoop. Straining his ears, he could hear nothing inside. So he took a chance and peeked through the window. The front office was empty, but there was an open doorway—where Frank could see the back of a tall, red-headed man in an ill-fitting police uniform. He stood over the body of another man in uniform, and he was holding a gun!

That did it. Frank knew his adversary was in there. And he had little time to spare. He would have one chance, and only one chance, to make good.

Sneaking behind the cruiser, Frank placed his economy-size Molotov cocktail on the ground. Then he jimmied open the trunk with the tire iron.

"Well, well," Frank said in surprise. The trunk wasn't empty as he'd expected. In fact, it was quite full—of a furious, squirming Officer Higgins! The highway patrolman was in his underwear, his arms and legs bound together, his mouth gagged. He looked like a trussed-up turkey, ready for the oven.

Higgins twisted and turned, trying to say something through the gag.

"It hasn't been your day, has it?" Frank said, reaching for him.

Frank lifted the heavy officer from the trunk and eased him to the ground.

Higgins began to roll in the dirt, emphatically demanding that Frank untie him. It was just as well the gag reduced his shouts to mere mumbles. Frank didn't want the hit man getting any warning.

Instead, he quickly pulled Higgins well clear of the car and left him leaning against the side of the building.

"Sorry about this, officer," Frank said, dashing back to the police cruiser. He placed his homemade bomb in the recently vacated trunk, on top of the car's gas tank. Then he ran to the front of the car, where he opened the hood and quickly removed the battery.

Placing the battery near the front stoop, he knelt down with the contacts for the jumper cables in his hands. "Not much of a detonator," he whispered. "I just hope it works."

Inside the small cell block, the hit man couldn't resist gloating over his triumph.

"You led me on a merry chase," he told Joe

and Rita. "But it's over. I've finally caught up with you."

Joe's face was a study in anger. He gripped the bars that held him in, yelling, "You dirty—"

"Call me Skell, kid." The hit man's thin lips creased in a smile. "It's just a nickname—but in my line of business, you don't give your real name away." The smile broadened. "Even if you make sure no witnesses will be left."

"I don't believe you," Joe said. "You're going to kill us—in a sheriff's office? Every lawman in Colorado will be after you."

The hit man shrugged. "By the time I finish, it will look accidental. Maybe a fire." He glanced around. "Or maybe something more artistic."

"You'll never get away with it."

"Famous last words, kid. Tomorrow, I'll be on a beach somewhere, relaxing in the sun." Skell smiled down at the fallen sheriff. "Yes, sir, everything's here in a neat package. All tight, just as he said."

Rita stood with her hands clenched around the strong iron bars of her cell. "*You* killed my father?" she whispered.

"That's my job. I'm the best." Skell tapped a finger to his skinny chest. "My employers knew when they hired me that the job was guaranteed." He looked at the two prisoners. "Even if the clean-up meant a lot of work."

Joe threw himself against his cell door—but it held without budging. "Come on," he taunted the hit man. "Make it a fair fight. How about you and me going hand to hand? No weapons, no tricks. And let the better man walk away!"

"Hey, I'm no hero," Skell said with a smirk. "I'm a businessman. Give it up, kid. You're history. I'm just enjoying a few minutes before I'm rid of you forever."

He checked the magazine of his riot gun. "Eight shells," he said. "Way more than I need. One shot for the brave fool. One for the little lady. A quick job. But you've made me a rich man, kids." His smile was knife thin, now.

"Yeah?" Joe countered. "How much are they paying you?"

"Good work doesn't come cheap," the hit man said. "But my employers knew that I'd make good on the contract. You," he added, pointing the shotgun at Joe, "will have to be a freebie."

"Quit torturing us," Joe said quietly. "If you're going to do it, then get it over with."

"I'm in no hurry," Skell said, throwing the shotgun over his shoulder. "You know what your problem is, kid? You've got a thick head. You don't know when to die. You should have bought it in the trunk of your car, back at Cripple Mine. Either you were lucky, or I was sloppy. Either way, I'll clean it up now. But I'll try to make it quick. After all, I owe you some thanks on this job."

"You owe *me* some thanks?" Joe echoed.

The hit man nodded. "Sure do. You see, I

didn't know exactly where to find Tabor. But when I tracked you and Rita back to the cabin and saw 'Uncle Delbert,' well, I knew I'd found the right cabin. Sorry I couldn't get you there, but my gun was in my car up on the road. I knew I'd catch up with you, though.''

Joe glanced over at Rita. "I'm sorry," he said miserably. "I blew it. I blew everything."

Rita took his hand through the bars and squeezed it. "It's all right," she whispered. "It wasn't your fault. You tried to help."

"Hey, I hate to cut this touching scene short, but, well, business is business," Skell cut in. He pulled a knife from his belt. "What do you think of this plan?" he asked Joe and Rita. "After I shoot you two, I'll get the boy's prints on this knife and then stick it into the sheriff."

He nodded happily. "When they find you, they'll piece together what must have happened. A tragic story. A punk stabbed the sheriff who, dying, somehow managed to shoot his attackers. Artistic, huh?"

Rita lost all control. "Your bosses may kill me, but they're all still in jail," she snapped. "And I'm glad of it."

"Yeah, well, they're in jail now," Skell admitted. "But there is the new trial. And without the star witnesses, my bosses can buy their way out of it. What do you think about that?"

"I think you're a real sick piece of work," Joe said.

Skell brought up his shotgun, his eyes cold as ice. "I was going to kill the little lady first, just so you could watch," he told Joe. "But I'm tired of your lip. You go first!"

Joe drew himself up as straight as he could, as did Rita in her cell.

"How pretty," the killer snarled. "Just like Romeo and Juliet. Okay, kids, the party's over!"

Skell's finger tightened on the trigger—and the whole room shook with a tremendous force!

Chapter

18

INSTINCTIVELY JOE HARDY closed his eyes. Then he opened them in surprise. He wasn't dead! What had happened?

He looked first at Rita, then at Skell. The explosion had thrown Skell against Joe's cell and he stood staring through the doorway into the front of the sheriff's office.

The place was destroyed. The explosion had shattered the windows, sending glass and debris sailing. Smoke was pouring in, and they could all hear the crackle of flames outside.

Joe tried to take advantage of the moment, grabbing for the barrel of the shotgun. But before he could get a solid grasp, Skell snarled and yanked the weapon away.

"I'll deal with you two later!" the hit man shouted, running to investigate the blast.

Skell charged into the office and went into a crouch behind the sheriff's desk. But it took him a moment to realize that the explosion had come from *outside* the building. Holding the shotgun in one hand and Higgins's stolen service revolver in his other hand, he crept to the window for a view.

Even in the back room, Joe could hear Skell cursing.

Quickly the hit man moved to the front door, kicking it open. Smoke came billowing into the office, carrying the stench of burning gasoline. Firing the revolver, Skell plunged into the smoke, toward the spot where he'd left the patrol car.

Crouched low on the porch beside the front steps, Frank watched the hit man rush past him. As soon as he saw the hit man disappear into the billowing cloud of smoke, Frank dashed inside the sheriff's office.

There was no time to congratulate himself, even though it seemed that the diversion had worked. Frank grabbed the sheriff's keys from the desk and ran to the cells in the back. He had a suspicion who he'd find there.

Holding a finger to his lips, Frank leapt over the prone sheriff and quickly unlocked the door to Joe's cell.

"The hit man will be back in a moment," Frank whispered. "Stay where you are. We'll get the drop on him together."

Joe stared in amazement. Maybe the shock of almost dying had cut through the tangle of half memories in his head. Now he realized who this dark-haired guy was. "Frank," Joe whispered. "You're my brother, Frank."

Frank glanced up and grinned. "Well, it's about time! I was getting pretty tired of being the Hardy Boy. Let's put an end to this whole mess."

"And how!" Joe said.

Frank was just about to unlock Rita's cell when he heard the hit man returning. He had only a moment to dive back into the front room and under the sheriff's desk.

Skell holstered the pistol and used his free hand to clear the smoke from in front of him. Frank held his breath, as he watched Skell's boots move past him, marching toward the cells.

"I don't have time to fool around now!" Skell's face was twisted in a snarl. "Somehow, the patrol car has exploded. I'm finishing this job and getting out of here!"

The hit man took a step toward Joe's cell and leveled the shotgun. "So long, kid."

Joe's foot shot out, kicking his cell door open right in Skell's face! A shotgun blast ripped into the ceiling as the hit man staggered back.

Frank scrambled free from the desk and jumped Skell from behind. But even though Skell was skinny, he had wiry strength and agility. As soon as he felt Frank's weight, he ducked and sent Frank spilling over him. Skell reared back, ready to club Frank with the butt of the shotgun.

But Joe came charging out of his cell, plowing into Skell's belly.

The tackle sent the hit man tumbling backward.

Joe followed up, lifting the hit man to his feet. He swung both fists into Skell's chest. Then he grabbed for the shotgun, trying to wrestle it from the killer's grasp.

But Skell wasn't finished yet. He smashed the gun down on his knee, breaking Joe's hold. Then he threw a solid punch to Joe's jaw, sending him whirling back until he crashed against Rita's cell.

Rita helped the cause by pushing Joe back toward the action.

Both Hardys came at Skell from different directions—Frank in a classic karate stance, Joe with his fists up.

But the killer still had the upper hand—he still had the shotgun. Ramming the butt into Joe's stomach, he swung the barrel wildly, clearing some room for himself. Joe and Frank had to jump back.

"Cute. But not cute enough." Skell's lips were a thin, angry line.

"It's two against one," Frank told him. "Put the gun down."

"Two against one doesn't count—not when I can blow you away!" Skell swung the shotgun again at Joe, who ducked from the blow, moving toward Frank.

"Don't get too close to me," Frank hissed. "We can't let him take us out with one shot!"

Skell twisted around, aiming the gun at Frank. His face registered surprise as Frank's foot lashed out at his chest. But the hit man met the threat, clubbing Frank's leg with the shotgun barrel. Joe circled round, trying for another attack.

Working as a team, the Hardys closed in on Skell. He began to back-pedal, bringing up the gun again. "Okay, who wants it first?" the hit man said, quickly shifting his aim from Frank to Joe, then back to Frank.

His eyes were locked on the brothers now. If Frank or Joe took a step forward, Skell was ready to shoot.

He stepped back to get a little more distance from his attackers—and crashed into Rita's cell.

Rita's hand darted through the bars to snatch the service revolver from his holster, jabbing it into Skell's back.

"Hold it right there," she warned.

The hit man was taken by surprise. He stiffened, half turning his head. Frank was ready to take advantage of that lapse. He clubbed both fists down on the shotgun, knocking it from Skell's hands.

Even as Frank was attacking, Joe unleashed an uppercut that sent the killer's skull crashing against the iron bars, knocking him out.

Skell slumped to the floor, and Joe drew back for another punch. Frank grabbed Joe's arm and felt the muscles tensing under his fingers.

"Stop it!" Frank shouted. "That's enough!"

"No, it isn't!" Joe shouted, trying to pull free. "This guy's a killer, Frank!"

"Then he'll face charges in a proper court of law," Frank insisted, barely holding Joe back.

Joe's fury began to ease. "You're right," he told Frank. "I guess I just forgot who I was for a moment."

"For a moment?" Frank said with a grin. He released Joe's arm and patted his brother on the back. "It's good to have you back, Joe."

Joe found the keys and unlocked the door to Rita's cell. She stepped out, and began to break down, her body shaking and tears falling freely down her face.

"It's over. It's all over now, Rita," Joe said softly. He removed the pistol from her hand and drew her close.

She leaned against him and wiped her eyes. "Yes. You even know who you really are, now."

Frank stepped forward and smiled. "This may seem like a weird time for introductions—but I'm Frank Hardy." Gesturing toward Joe, he added, "This is my younger brother, Joe."

By the time the sheriff finally came to, he thought he was still dreaming. Hovering over him were Frank, Joe, and Rita. Officer Higgins, back in his uniform, was on the telephone, calling his headquarters. And behind bars was Skell, handcuffed to the steel frame of a cell cot.

The sheriff jumped up with a fierce look. "Someone had better have a good explanation for all this!"

Frank and Joe chuckled.

Officer Higgins hung up the phone. "Well, sheriff, it's this way." He quickly brought the local lawman up to date, carefully avoiding some of the more humiliating things that had happened to him in the course of the adventure. "These kids cut a lot of corners," he finally finished. "Blowing up my patrol car is a serious offense." He grudgingly continued. "But they did pull the fat out of the fire. For *all* of us."

The sheriff still looked pretty embarrassed. "That guy sure got the jump on me. But then, I usually think a man in uniform is on my side." He shook hands with Frank. "Thanks for coming along when you did."

Then he turned to Joe and Rita. "Guess I owe you two more than thanks—you deserve an apology."

Joe nodded. "At least it's all over now."

"Pretty soon, you'll be heading home," Higgins cut in. "Headquarters told me that your dad is in Denver, hopping a helicopter to get here."

"Dad!" said Joe. "I forgot about him!"

"You forgot about a lot of stuff," Frank said with a laugh. "But I think Dad will be glad to find you all in one piece."

Joe went over to Rita, who was standing outside the door to the office, staring at the wreckage of patrol car 28. He understood her silence. The terror would not be over for her. Skell was in custody. But she'd lost her father, and her hiding place. The criminals would be after her until she testified—and maybe afterward for revenge.

"Come with us," Joe told her. "You'll be safe in Bayport."

"I'd like to think so," Rita said, sadly shaking her head. "I'd enjoy getting to know you better. But I can't."

She took a long, deep breath. "I'm going back into the witness protection program." She clasped Joe's hand. "Not because I want to go. Because I *have* to go."

Joe nodded numbly. "So this is goodbye, then. I'll never see you again."

She kissed him, her eyes shining with tears. "Never say never, Joe."

As they drew apart, Joe could hear the clattering sound of a helicopter approaching. "Hey, Frank," he called inside. "I think our ride is coming."

"Great," said Frank, coming to the door. "Just promise me one thing."

Joe looked puzzled. "What?"

Frank grinned. "Whatever you do, don't hit your head climbing aboard. You can be a dangerous enemy—and I don't want you trying to push me out of that chopper at two thousand feet!"

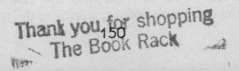
Thank you for shopping
The Book Rack

Frank and Joe's next case:

How can a man steal millions and millions from a company—and then disappear? That's what the Hardys have to find out or a friend's father will take the rap.

What they discover is the ultimate getaway—an escape plot that defies imagination. Frank and Joe set off on the same trail, with a briefcase full of hot bills. It leads them to a tropical hideaway. But as the Hardys learn, this is no paradise.

Can they blow the secret of this escape route? Or will they get blown away themselves? Find out in *Perfect Getaway*, Case #12 in The Hardy Boys Casefiles.

HAVE YOU SEEN THE HARDY BOYS® LATELY?

THE HARDY BOYS © CASE FILES

#1 DEAD ON TARGET 67258/$2.75

#2 EVIL, INC. 67259/$2.75

#3 CULT OF CRIME 67260/$2.75

#4 THE LAZARUS PLOT 62129/$2.75

#5 EDGE OF DESTRUCTION 62646/$2.75

#6 THE CROWNING TERROR 62647/$2.75

#7 DEATHGAME 62648/$2.75

#8 SEE NO EVIL 62649/$2.75

#9 THE GENIUS THIEVES 63080/$2.75

#10 HOSTAGES OF HATE 63081/$2.75

#11 BROTHER AGAINST BROTHER 63082/$2.75

#12 PERFECT GETAWAY 63083/$13.75

#13 THE BORGIA DAGGER 64463/$2.75

#14 TOO MANY TRAITORS 64460/$2.75

#15 BLOOD RELATIONS 64461/$2.75

#16 LINE OF FIRE 64462/$2.75

Simon & Schuster, Mail Order Dept. ASD
200 Old Tappan Rd., Old Tappan, N.J. 07675

Please send me the books I have checked above. I am enclosing $_____ (please add 75¢ to cover postage and handling for each order. N.Y.S. and N.Y.C. residents please add appropriate sales tax). Send check or money order—no cash or C.O.D.'s please. Allow up to six weeks for delivery. For purchases over $10.00 you may use VISA: card number, expiration date and customer signature must be included.

Name _____

Address _____

City _____ State/Zip _____

VISA Card No. _____ Exp. Date _____

Signature _____ 120-05

FROM THE CREATORS OF NANCY DREW®
AN EXCITING NEW ADVENTURE SERIES

The Linda Craig Adventures™
By Ann Sheldon

Linda Craig lives on beautiful Rancho Del Sol in Southern California. It's the perfect place for a young gifted rider and her horse—especially one like Amber. A high-spirited golden palomino, Amber is the smartest and most wonderful horse a girl could ever hope for. As a team, it seems Amber and Linda can do just about anything, as they ride all around Rancho Del Sol—finding action and excitement at every turn.

Join Linda and Amber as they ride the trail to fun and adventure in:

☐ ### The Golden Secret

Rancho Del Sol has been in Linda's family for generations. But now the ranch is in trouble. Unless Linda's family can produce the missing deed to the ranch, they'll be forced to leave. In the attic Linda finds a clue to the missing deed in an old song called "The Golden Secret." Its mysterious words lead her to an abandoned gold mine and danger—only Amber can help her now.

☐ ### A Star For Linda

It's Fiesta Day in Lockwood, and Linda has been chosen to act as sheriff of the posse that chases the stolen stage and brings back its cargo of "gold," in the annual "stagecoach robbery." The robbery goes as planned, but the stagecoach has vanished into thin air. Linda, with the help of Amber and her friends, is more determined than ever to find out who has stolen the missing rig—no matter what the danger.

DON'T MISS A NEW LINDA CRAIG ADVENTURE EVERY OTHER MONTH!
The Linda Craig Adventures is a trademark of Simon & Schuster, Inc.

Simon & Schuster Mail Order Dept.
200 Old Tappan Rd., Old Tappan, N.J. 07675

Please send me the books I have checked above. I am enclosing $_____ (please add 75¢ to cover postage and handling for each order. N.Y.S. and N.Y.C. residents please add appropriate sales tax). Send check or money order--no cash or C.O.D.'s please. Allow up to six weeks for delivery. For purchases over $10.00 you may use VISA: card number, expiration date and customer signature must be included.

Name _____

Address _____

City _____ State/Zip _____

VISA Card No. _____ Exp. Date _____

Signature _____ 158-01

HAVE YOU SEEN
NANCY DREW®
LATELY?

THE NANCY DREW FILES™

1 SECRETS CAN KILL 64193/$2.75
2 DEADLY INTENT 64393/$2.75
3 MURDER ON ICE 64194/$2.75
4 SMILE AND SAY MURDER 64585/$2.75
5 HIT AND RUN HOLIDAY 64394/$2.75
6 WHITE WATER TERROR 64586/$2.75
7 DEADLY DOUBLES 62543/$2.75
8 TWO POINTS FOR MURDER 63079/$2.75
9 FALSE MOVES 63076/$2.75
#10 BURIED SECRETS 63077/$2.75
#11 HEART OF DANGER 63078/$2.75
#12 FATAL RANSOM 62644/$2.75
#13 WINGS OF FEAR 64137/ $2.75
#14 THIS SIDE OF EVIL 64139/$2.75
#15 TRIAL BY FIRE 64139/$2.75
#16 NEVER SAY DIE 64140/$2.75
#17 STAY TUNED FOR DANGER 64141/$2.75
#18 CIRCLE OF EVIL 64142/$2.75
#19 SISTERS IN CRIME 64225/$2.75
#20 VERY DEADLY YOURS 64226/$2.75
#21 RECIPE FOR MURDER 64227/$2.75
#22 FATAL ATTRACTION 64228/$2.75
#23 SINISTER PARADISE 64229/$2.75
#24 TILL DEATH DO US PART
64230/$2.75

Simon & Schuster, Mail Order Dept. ASB
200 Old Tappan Rd., Old Tappan, N.J. 07675

Please send me the books I have checked above. I am enclosing $_____ (please add 75¢ to cover postage and handling for each order. N.Y.S. and N.Y.C. residents please add appropriate sales tax). Send check or money order—no cash or C.O.D.'s please. Allow up to six weeks for delivery. For purchases over $10.00 you may use VISA: card number, expiration date and customer signature must be included.

Name _____

Address _____

City _____ State/Zip _____

VISA Card No. _____ Exp. Date _____

Signature _____ 119-04